BASEBALL
GREAT

BAS
GR

HarperCollins*Publishers*

Special thanks to Dickie Woodridge and Bud Poliquin

Baseball Great

Copyright © 2009 by Tim Green

Printed in the U.S.A.

Library of Congress Cataloging-in-Publication Data is available.

ISBN 978-0-06-162686-9 (trade bdg.) – ISBN 978-0-06-162687-6 (lib. bdg.)

Typography by Joel Tippie

1 2 3 4 5 6 7 8 9 10

❖

First Edition

For my beautiful girls, Illyssa, Tessa, and Tate

CHAPTER ONE

JOSH WONDERED WHY EVERY time something really good happened, something else had to spoil it. It had been like this since he could remember, like biting into a ruby red apple only to find a brown worm crawling through the crisp, white fruit. For the first time since he'd moved to his new neighborhood, he had been recognized, and his unusual talent had been appreciated. So why was it that that same fame had kicked up the muddy rumor that got a high school kid looking to bash his teeth in?

For the moment, though, riding the school bus, he was safe. The school newspaper in Josh's backpack filled his whole body with an electric current of joy and pride, so much so that his cheeks burned. He sat alone in the very front seat and kept his eyes ahead, ignoring the stares and whispers as the other kids got off at the earlier stops. When Jaden Neidermeyer, the new girl from Texas who'd written the article, got off at her stop, Josh stared hard at his sneakers. He just couldn't look.

After she left, he glanced around and carefully parted the lips of his backpack's zipper. Without removing the newspaper, he stole another glance at the headline, BASEBALL GREAT, and the picture of him with a bat and the caption underneath: "Grant Middle's best hope for its first-ever citywide championship, Josh LeBlanc."

The bus ground to a halt at his stop and Josh got off.

As the bus rumbled away, Josh saw Bart Wilson standing on the next corner. The tenth grader pitched his cigarette into the gutter and started toward him with long strides. Josh gasped, turned, and ran without looking back. A car blared its horn. Brakes squealed. Josh leaped back, his heart galloping fast, like the tenth grader now heading his way, even faster. Josh circled the car—the driver yelling at him through the window—and dashed across the street and down the far sidewalk.

He rounded the corner at Murphy's bar and sprinted up the block, ducking behind a wrecked station wagon at Calhoon's Body Shop, peeking through the broken web of glass back toward the corner. Breathing hard, he slipped the straps of the backpack he carried around his shoulders and fastened it tight. Two men in hooded sweatshirts and jeans jackets burst out of Murphy's and got into a pickup truck; otherwise, Josh saw no one. Still, he scooted up the side street, checking behind him and dodging from one parked car to another for cover.

When he saw his home, a narrow, red two-story place with a steep roof and a sagging front porch, he breathed deep, and his heart began to slow. The previous owner had three pit bulls, and so a chain-link fence surrounded the house and its tiny front and back lawns, separating them from the close-packed neighbors on either side. The driveway ran tight to the house, and like the single, detached garage, it was just outside the fence. Josh lifted the latch, but as he pulled open the front gate, a hand appeared from nowhere, slamming it shut. The latch clanked home, and the hand spun Josh around.

"What you running from?" asked Bart Wilson, the tenth-grade smoker.

CHAPTER TWO

"I'M NOT," JOSH SAID, his heart dancing in his throat.

Bart leaned up against the gate, blocking Josh's path to the front door and folding his arms across his chest. He stood nearly six feet tall—no bigger than Josh, with arms and legs skinny as a spider's—but his big, crooked teeth, shaggy hair, and snake tattoo crawling among the veins on his arm scared Josh silly.

"You think you're something, don't you?" Bart asked.

"No."

"Then why you talking to Sheila? She's my girl."

"I'm not," Josh said, his eyes flickering up at his house, half hoping to see someone to help him and the other half hoping to avoid the embarrassment of being bullied.

4

"She says."

"She sat next to me at lunch is all," Josh said.

"I'm here to kick your teeth in," Bart said, standing tall and reaching out to give Josh a poke in the chest.

"I don't want to fight," Josh said.

"You have to," Bart said, balling up his fists.

"No," Josh said. "I don't want to."

"Come on," Bart said, giving him a shove. "You're gonna fight me."

"No," Josh said, shaking his head and looking down at his feet. "I don't want any trouble."

"You should have thought of that when you started going after my girl."

"I'm not."

"You're some baseball hotshot, I hear," Bart said. "You think you're cool?"

"No."

"'Cause you're not."

CHAPTER THREE

JOSH SAID NOTHING, BUT he began to back away. When he got to the corner of the fence, he sprinted up the driveway, away from the tenth grader and the fight. His mom popped out the back door and he ran smack into her at the side gate and spilling the bag of garbage she meant to take to the trash cans beside the garage.

"Josh!" she said. "What?"

Josh glanced back, expecting Bart's menacing face but seeing only an empty driveway.

"Hi, Mom," he said. "I'll take care of that for you."

"Thank you," his mom said, but her voice sounded distant and her eyes swam with worry. She twisted her hands up in her apron. "I'll . . . I'll see you inside."

His mom flung open the door and disappeared. Josh wrinkled his brow but sighed and bent down. He picked up the bag, stuffing the garbage back inside before taking it out to the trash can. Through one of the dusty square windows in the garage door, Josh noticed that his father's car sat inside the garage. His stomach twisted into a fresh knot.

He took slow steps back toward the house, thinking of what it could mean.

The only other time Josh had seen his father home from work during baseball season had been to announce a move. Nothing but that or a game could take his father out of the daily routine of practice. In Josh's twelve years they'd moved six times, and, despite Bart Wilson, Josh didn't want to move again. He didn't have a lot of friends, but he'd never had a better one than Benji Lido, and he expected once baseball season began tomorrow, he'd begin to have a lot more.

The screen door had no screen, but its metal frame still guarded the cracked wooden door that led to the kitchen. He swung them both open, one after the other, and stepped inside. In the corner, his little sister lay asleep in her playpen, rolled up in her favorite blanket with a thumb in her mouth. His mother sat at the small, round kitchen table with a cup of coffee in front of her, still clutching her apron. Next to her sat his dad, a big, square-shouldered man with jet black hair who made the wooden chair and, in fact, the whole room seem smaller.

In his father's ham-sized hand was the lucky baseball

he'd used to throw the no-hitter in the Pennsylvania High School State Championship. It was the game, his father always said, that had made him the seventeenth player selected in the Major League Baseball draft, the game whose celebration led to Josh's birth, and to his parents' being married. As Josh watched the ball—worn smooth and shiny through years of worry—roll in his father's huge, undulating hand, he also felt a pang of embarrassment that dwarfed what he'd felt on the school bus.

Neither of his parents noticed him. They both stared up at the phone on the wall beside the stove, waiting for news that Josh knew couldn't be good.

CHAPTER FOUR

WHEN HIS FATHER FINALLY noticed Josh, his thick, black eyebrows gathered low over his dark eyes, adding to the stormy look on his face.

"Thought you had practice," his father said in a voice that rumbled like distant thunder.

"Tomorrow," Josh said, going to the refrigerator, pouring himself a glass of milk, and tearing open a pack of frozen Fig Newtons as if nothing was wrong.

"Well," his father said, with a glance at Josh's mother, "this is it. It's got to be."

His mother offered a hopeful smile.

"But we don't know," his father said, still rumbling with the ball now clutched tight in his fist. "We never know. It's never in till it's in, and it's never out till it's out; that's the game."

Josh nodded at the logic. He knew now that even though the call they waited for might take them away, it would also fulfill his father's lifelong dream. Despite being the seventeenth overall pick of the draft and being heralded as the young lefty who'd save the Mets, Josh's father had never thrown a single major-league pitch in his twelve years as a pro. Instead, he had bounced around from one small city to another, riddling the countryside with his left-handed prowess, up and down the minor leagues in four different organizations but never quite making it beyond Triple-A ball.

"Vasquez tore a hamstring," his father said, biting back a smile and looking grim. "Soon as I heard that, I had to get out of the clubhouse. Wanted to get the news right here with my family."

Josh knew his baseball, especially the players in his father's organization. He could recite each player's batting average and each pitcher's ERA for the past three seasons. Armand Vasquez was the Toronto Blue Jays' second left-handed relief pitcher, limiting hitters to a batting average of .209. Josh's father threw for the Syracuse Chiefs, Toronto's Triple-A farm team.

His father issued a nervous chuckle and said, "I mean, how do you not bring up last year's MVP when he's on track to do it again? When you've got an ERA of—"

"One-point-eight-seven," Josh's mother said in a burst of numbers, her high, round cheeks turning candy apple red.

His father nodded and said, "So."

Josh bit into his cookie, nodding along with them, and, as if on cue, the phone rang.

His father jumped up, snatching it from the wall.

CHAPTER FIVE

JOSH'S FATHER SLAMMED THE phone back onto its hook and glared at Josh and his mom.

"Won't tell me a dang thing," his father said. "You believe that? My whole life in the balance and Simmons says he needs to see me in person. If I knew that, I wouldn't have left the stadium. Come on, Josh. I want you to be there. I did most of this for you anyway."

Josh opened his mouth to say it didn't matter to him if his dad ever threw a pitch in the big leagues or not, but the look on his father's face made him think better of it.

"I'll get that," his mother said, taking the empty milk glass from his hand and bringing it to the sink. "You go with your father."

"Sure," Josh said, and followed the big man out of

the house and into the garage without speaking.

They rode in silence, his father chomping a wad of gum and changing the radio station every couple seconds and Josh biting his tongue to keep from asking him to stop. In minutes the street broke the rise and they could see the stadium spread out below, pinned in on all sides, by the highway, the train station, a swamp, and several blocks of abandoned warehouses. As they descended the hill and turned the corner, the central entrance of the stadium rose up like the tower of a fortress. A flag flew from its peak. An iron fence surrounded the players' parking lot, and Josh's dad pulled in to the mixed bag of cars. Some, like their Taurus, were late-model clunkers. Only the new rookies with signing bonuses drove shiny sports cars or gleaming SUVs.

At the side door, a sleepy man wearing thick glasses and a windbreaker with a security patch read the paper without looking up.

"Hey, Glen," Josh's father said.

"Uh-huh," Glen said, licking a finger and turning the page.

Josh stayed close, following his dad through the maze of hallways, past where they would turn for the lockers, to the end of a hall and into the elevator.

The general manager's office had a back wall of glass overlooking the nearby lake and the smokestacks of several power plants and a steel mill on the far shore. Josh knew the GM but had never been in his office before, and it surprised him to see that Dallas Simmons sat with his desk facing the double doors instead of the panoramic view. Dallas had white tufts of hair over his ears, but he looked young for an old guy. His skin, the color of coffee with lots of milk, ran smoothly from the top of his head to the base of his neck without a wrinkle. His hazel eyes normally twinkled like Santa Claus's, dueling with the flash of white teeth in his easy smile.

When he saw Josh, the light in Dallas's eyes went out. Still, the GM cranked up a smile and said, "Josh, good to see you. Start your season yet?"

"Tomorrow," Josh said. "Good to see you, too."

"Future Hall of Famer," Josh's dad said, patting him on the back.

"Gary," Dallas said, addressing Josh's dad, "maybe Josh can help field some balls? I've got that kid from Tulsa doing some extra hitting out on the field."

Josh's dad gave Dallas a funny look, and his hand went around the back of Josh's neck. "No, that's okay. He'll stay."

"Because I'd love to have him see this kid hit," Dallas said, clearing his throat and nodding toward the door.

"Say what you gotta say, Dallas," his father said in a growl. "They're bringing me up, right?"

Dallas looked at Josh's father for what seemed like

a long time before he sighed and pinched the top of his nose. Shaking his head, he said, "No, Gary, they're not."

"I'm a lefty," his father said softly.

"I know," Dallas said.

"Your MVP," his father said.

"They want to take a look at Dick Campbell."

"Campbell stinks!" his father said. "His ERA is what? Four-point-six-three? You're joking."

"They think he translates."

"*He* translates?"

"He's twenty years old," Dallas said, looking up wearily, avoiding Josh's eyes. "They think he's got potential, and he does. You're thirty-one."

Josh's father stepped up to Dallas's big, wide desk, placing his large hands flat on its dark, grainy surface like two skillets. He leaned toward the GM.

"You tell those butt heads in Toronto that they either bring me up," his father said coldly, jutting out his chin at the GM, "or they can go find the Chiefs another MVP."

Dallas rested an elbow on the desk and dropped his forehead into his hands.

"Don't say that," Dallas said, wagging his head in despair.

"When you're down," his father said, "you hit where it hurts."

"They don't care," Dallas said slowly.

"It's like a poker game," Josh's father said. "I've played it before. They like to bluff."

"It's no bluff, Gary. They thought about it. They know how well you've done, but bringing in a one-point-eight-seven ERA against Rochester isn't like doing it against the Yankees. You can't go up, and you can't go back down."

His father stared hard at Dallas and said, "I wouldn't expect you to say anything else."

"I tried, Gary," Dallas said, looking up at him. "I begged them."

"Well," his father said, looking back uncomfortably at Josh, "next time. We know what that's like; don't we, buddy?"

Josh nodded enthusiastically.

"No, Gary," Dallas said. "I'm sorry. It's over."

"What's over?" his father said, standing tall and clenching his fists.

"They agreed to let me keep you through next week," Dallas said, "to play out the home series with Pawtucket. They're letting me have a retirement ceremony during the seventh-inning stretch. Saturday's bat day. There should be a crowd."

Josh's father did something Josh had never seen before, ever. He let his enormous shoulders sag. His chin dipped toward his chest, and one of his big hands swept over his face.

"I—" he said to Dallas, then stopped.

Josh thought he heard his father whisper that he was the MVP.

Outside Dallas's window the sun sparkled on the lake, and an army of puffy clouds marched across the sky. Josh's father brushed past him and flung open the office door. Dallas called to him, but Josh's father stood punching the elevator button, and Josh followed him. Dallas's secretary didn't look up from her typing as they waited for the elevator to come, and Dallas stopped calling so that when it did arrive, the ding of its bell sounded like the end of a prizefight.

Back in the car, Josh waited until they pulled into their own driveway before he asked, "Dad, what happens now?"

CHAPTER SIX

THE NEXT DAY, JOSH stuffed his baseball mitt, cleats, and hat into his gym locker. He felt someone tap his shoulder and he turned around.

"You see this, dude?" Benji asked, shoving the school newspaper into his face. Benji's straight brown hair fell across his face, his dark eyes glittering up at Josh. His plump cheeks tugged at a mischievous smile. Benji was average height but stout and tough, a good athlete who was quick to laugh himself but even quicker when it came to making other people laugh.

Josh felt his cheeks heat up. "Yeah, I saw it."

He pushed past Benji and out into the crowded hallway, making for the stairs and his book locker on the second floor before the first bell rang.

"Dude, this girl *loves* you," Benji said, following close.

"What girl?" Josh asked, turning around when he reached his locker, his mind on Sheila, the tenth grader's girlfriend.

"*This* girl," Benji said, stabbing his finger at the byline of the newspaper article about Josh. Benji closed his eyes, puckered his lips, and made kissing noises at Josh.

"Cut it out."

"She does."

"I got other things to worry about," Josh said, spinning the dial on his locker and choosing to tell Benji the next worst thing to his dad getting cut from the Chiefs. "Bart Wilson showed up at my bus stop yesterday after school wanting to fight me, because, he says, I'm after Sheila Conway and she's his girlfriend."

"Are you?" Benji asked.

Josh gave him a dirty look. "She sat next to me at lunch. You saw it. She's an eighth grader. What am I supposed to do?"

"Not keep smiling at her," Benji said.

"Believe me, I won't," Josh said, stuffing his backpack into the locker and removing the books he needed for the first two periods. "That's what you get for being nice."

"Anyway, you've got a new girlfriend now," Benji said, holding up the paper.

"Cut it out," Josh said, closing his locker and heading for homeroom.

"You do."

"I'll see you at lunch."

*　　*　　*

At lunch, Josh bought four milks, then found an empty table near the glass wall that looked out over the hallway. He took four sandwiches out of his bag and lined them up with an apple and some pretzels. They only got twenty-two minutes to eat, and it took all of that for Josh to put down everything he needed to stay fueled up. Benji, who wasn't small but who was nowhere near Josh's size, could eat his lunch in five minutes, leaving him plenty of time to talk, which he did, usually without pause.

The long table began to fill up. Several guys Josh knew who were going out for the baseball team sat across from him, and he said hello quietly, keeping his head angled down at his food. When Benji arrived, he whistled and hooted and slapped high fives with the other guys, asking them if they were ready for baseball season. Benji planned on being the team's catcher. Josh, like the others, listened as Benji told a story about how the baseball coach's wife divorced him after the team lost every single game last year.

"And I can't say I blame her, dude," Benji said. "No one likes a loser."

"That's not true, is it?" Josh asked, blinking at his friend.

"If it's not, it should be," Benji said, peeling back the paper on an enormous cupcake he pulled from his lunch bag.

"Speaking of divorce and marriage," Benji continued, slowly licking the colored sprinkles from the brown frosting, "you set a wedding date yet with Jaden Neidermeyer?"

The other kids laughed. Josh shook his head.

"Yeah," Benji said, dabbing the frosting now with his tongue, "any girl that writes an article like that is in love, deep."

Josh saw the kids across from them stop laughing suddenly. Their eyes went past Benji. He turned just in time to see Jaden, her face red and pinched, reach over Benji's shoulder and grab his hand.

Before Benji could react, Jaden slammed the cupcake up into his face, mashing it around and leaving him with a mask of brown frosting and yellow hunks of cake.

The entire table howled with laughter. Benji, to his credit, sat calmly, licking a clean spot around his mouth.

"I love the *game,* you goober," Jaden said, her voice tinged with a southern accent as she scowled at Josh, "not *him.*"

"What did I do?" Josh asked.

"Nothing," she said in her light drawl. "You just sat there like a big dummy, listening to him talk about me when all I did was tell everybody how great a player you are. You know how much research I had to do? Tracking down your coach from when you lived in Manchester?

Going through all those stupid Little League records in Mr. O'Dwyer's basement that smells like cat crap?"

Josh's mouth fell open. He stared.

Jaden had light brown skin and long, frizzy hair that she kept pulled into a ponytail. Except for big green eyes, which reminded Josh of a cat's, her features were small, almost elfish, even though she was one of the taller girls and big-boned. She was both pretty and formidable. She didn't have more than a handful of friends, and she rarely talked except to answer questions in class. But Josh thought that Jaden only *seemed* like a loner because she always had her nose in a book and hadn't moved into town much more than a year ago. Deep down, he suspected she was like a treasure box, and, if you lifted the lid, you'd be blinded by gems.

"I'm a reporter," Jaden said, jabbing a finger in the back of Benji's neck, "not a floozy."

Just then Josh saw Sheila Conway walking his way with a tray. Her long blond hair swished from side to side, glimmering. She wore a short black dress and a wide smile. Josh swallowed hard and looked up at Jaden.

"Would you mind sitting here?" he asked her, pulling out the empty chair beside him. "Please? I'll explain. I really need you to."

"Hey, dude," Benji said, dabbing some frosting out from the corner of his eye and licking his finger, "she just smashed a cupcake into my face and you're asking her to sit down?"

"Please," Josh said again, begging.

Jaden glanced over her shoulder and saw Sheila Conway coming. Jaden nodded her head and sat right down, smiling up at the older girl. Sheila wrinkled her nose, cast Josh a dirty look, and kept on going. Josh sighed and stole a glance at her as she strutted away.

"Thanks," he said to Jaden.

"Now you can leave," Benji said, leaning forward so Jaden could see his frown. His eyes popped out at her, unblinking in the mess of frosting. "Girls, they're nothing but trouble."

"Is he always this idiotic?" Jaden asked, taking an orange from her lunch bag and beginning to peel away the skin.

"You'll get used to it," Josh said, grinning and extending his hand.

Jaden returned the smile, and they shook.

CHAPTER SEVEN

JOSH SPRINTED OUT ONTO the baseball diamond, leaving the algebra equations, frog dissections, Greek myths, and important WWII dates behind. A warm breeze tugged at his hat. The smooth insides of the glove caressed his hand. His cleats punched clean holes in the fresh turf. From his back pocket, he extracted a pack of Big Red—the gum his dad chewed—and shucked three sticks free, one-handed, shoving them into his mouth to create a wad worthy of the day.

Instead of standing around like the others, he found his spot between second and third and stood, toes in the dirt, heels digging into the lip of the grass. They wanted him to pitch. At just under six feet and weighing 160 pounds, he was by far the biggest kid on the team. He could throw more heat than anyone, even the eighth graders, but pitching wasn't his gift—reaction time was. He could go places as a shortstop, and that's where he needed to play. His dad said so, and his dad was a pro.

Not anymore he's not.

The words came at him like the shriek from some heckler in the stands. Josh looked around, wondering if Benji or any of his other teammates had said it.

No one had said it, though.

The other boys stood in a small circle by the dugout, watching Benji play hot hands with their pitcher, Kerry Eschelman, crooning at the sound of the slaps and crying for blood.

Josh breathed easy. While the end of his dad's career created an unpleasant tension at home, it had its upside. They wouldn't have to move to Toronto, or back to Manchester, where the Double-A team was. Josh was tired of moving. Even though Benji could be a pain, Josh couldn't imagine middle school without him.

A whistle sounded, and Coach Miller yelled, "All right, bring it in!"

Josh jogged to the backstop with the rest of the kids. The coach counted the guys and told them that, unfortunately, everyone wouldn't make the team. Sixteen was the number he would carry. That meant six would go home. Josh looked around, knowing he had to make it but thinking of his dad's words about never being in until you're in. His dad was the team MVP, and he was out.

Josh set his jaw and punched a fist into his glove. He'd make it impossible for the coach to cut him.

Sometime during agility drills and stretching, Jaden arrived. One minute the small bleachers stood empty, the next she sat there with a little notebook and a pen, examining the field and the players as if they were fish in an aquarium. After short tosses, long tosses, and some infield drills, Coach Miller called them together again and said he wanted to see what they had in the way of offense.

"LeBlanc," Coach Miller said, pointing at Josh with a bat. "I hear you're gonna be our big star."

Josh looked down at his cleats and nudged the baseline with his toe.

"A baseball *great*?" Coach Miller said, chuckling and shaking his head. "You're a little young for that, don't you think?"

Josh's face felt as if it were on fire. He shrugged his shoulders, pulled on his batting glove, and grabbed the bat. When he had the rubber grip in his hands, the embarrassment melted away. He swung the bat slowly, feeling its weight, allowing his mind to wrap itself around the shape, making it part of him, an extension of his own arms and hands. Coach Miller barked out positions for the boys, telling Kerry to take the mound.

"Okay, LeBlanc," the coach said in a skeptical tone. "Let's see some greatness."

CHAPTER EIGHT

"COACH, COACH, COACH," BENJI said, stepping between Josh and Coach Miller and turning his cap around as he tugged on a batting glove. "You gotta let me go first, Coach. I'm gonna be your leadoff batter anyway, and you gotta let Eschelman warm up his arm on me, save the real stuff for our big bat."

Benji took the bat from Josh's hands. Coach Miller looked at Benji with an open mouth, as if he couldn't believe it. Benji didn't blink; he just stepped up to the plate.

"C'mon, Coach," Benji said, looking over his shoulder as he took some warm-up swings. "You can't win a championship standing around."

The coach took his clipboard and stood over to the side, then said to Kerry, "Go ahead, start throwing."

27

"*You* be on deck," Coach Miller said, pointing his pen at Josh and reasserting his authority.

Josh studied Kerry's motion as he wound up for the pitch. He watched the ball zip past Benji, who took a monster swing, connecting with nothing but air.

"Getting warm, getting warm," Benji said, holding off the next pitch with his left hand while he kicked dirt from his cleats and waved the bat in little circles with his right.

The next pitch came in, a curveball. Benji swung big again, nipping the ball and sending it dribbling down the third-base line.

"Nice hit," Coach Miller said, "for a bunt."

Benji stayed focused, swinging big every time, mostly whiffing and, if not, dribbling the ball into the infield or popping it up for an easy out.

"Okay, Lido," Coach Miller said. "That's all the lead-off batting I can take. Get out into right field and send Brandon in here."

"Coach, you gotta give me one more," Benji said. "Just one. One and done, Coach. One and done. Forget leadoff, I'm a heavy hitter, too. Come on, Eschelman; put one in here, you sissy."

Benji wiggled his cleats into the dirt. The pitch came fast, and he smacked it right over the center-field fence.

"Wahoo!" he screamed, pumping his fists in the air as he dropped the bat and jogged toward right field.

"Heavy hitter! Heavy hitter!"

Coach Miller chuckled, made some notes, and pointed to Josh.

"Now, let's see what you got," he said.

Josh hefted the bat, letting his body absorb its weight again. He studied the pitcher. In the article Jaden had written about Josh being a baseball great, the next biggest reason she said the team would win the championship was the pitching of Kerry Eschelman. Esch, as his friends called him, had pitched two no-hitters in Little League as a sixth grader. Josh saw why when he watched Esch pitch to Benji. There weren't many twelve-year-olds who could throw heat, and a curveball, and a changeup, too. That kind of pitching wasn't typical until high school.

But Josh wasn't worried.

The thing he had—reaction time, or reflex, or whatever it was called—that thing that never let a ball get by him in the infield, also let him see the ball the instant it left the pitcher's hand. He didn't just see it; he could *read* it. The placement of the hand, the laces on the ball, and the spin it had all showed up in his mind as clear as the headlines of a newspaper. And then he had the eye-hand coordination to smack it dead center with his bat.

So when Esch wound up and let fly with a curveball, Josh watched it come down the middle and veer toward the outside corner of the plate the way most people follow the path of a ladybug slogging along on a windowpane. He swung down on it, driving it right through the hole between first and second. Esch threw two more curves and a changeup, and Josh drove them into every hole the infield had.

The next pitch came in with heat, right down the pipe, Esch trying to burn one past. Josh jumped all over it, driving it over the left-field fence. Coach Miller let a low whistle escape his puckered lips. Josh glanced at him and tried not to smile.

"Let's see you put it past him again," Coach Miller said to Esch.

The pitcher threw three more fastballs in a row, and Josh put every one of them over the fence.

"I don't suppose you can bunt," Coach Miller said, almost under his breath.

Josh dribbled the next two pitches down the third-base line, stepping expertly in front of the pitch, his hands gingerly holding the bat as if it were a big potato chip.

Up in the bleachers, Jaden was on her feet, clapping politely at the show. Josh and Coach Miller grinned at each other.

That's when Josh's dad stepped out from behind the dugout. He wore a short leather coat. His hands were jammed into the pockets, and his face was darkened by unshaven stubble. He gave Josh a look that meant business and said, "Nice hitting, Son, but get your glove and come with me."

"Dad?" Josh asked. "Why?"

"I said, *get* your glove," his father growled through clenched teeth. "When I say do something, you don't ask why."

Josh dropped the bat and scooped up his glove, his eyes on the ground as he shuffled toward the dugout.

"Mr. LeBlanc," Coach Miller said, his voice sounding high and weak, almost apologetic, "Josh can't just leave. This first week of practice is to see who makes the team."

"Well, that's nice," Josh's father said, turning his red-rimmed eyes on Coach Miller, "but Josh doesn't need to make your team. He's not playing."

CHAPTER NINE

JOSH FELT LIKE A dog bone.

His dad was a pit bull, and he chewed and chewed.

Josh just sat there in the passenger seat, listening, knowing that he shouldn't have questioned his father, especially in front of another adult and especially when his father's pursuit of a lifelong dream had come to a grinding halt.

"I'm sorry," Josh said for the fourth time. "I'm sorry."

His father stared at the road, teeth clenched, hands white-knuckled on the wheel, driving steadily toward a place he hadn't yet revealed. It took a few minutes, but finally his thick eyebrows relaxed, his teeth disappeared behind his lips, and he took a deep breath that sounded like the filling of a big propane tank.

His father let the breath go and said, "Okay."

Now Josh waited, knowing not to ask. They got onto the highway and headed east, through the city and away from Onondaga Lake.

"You got talent, Josh," his father said. "Not just banging the ball around for some chump school team, real talent. When I was your age, no one did squat for me. My old man was a drunk. The only thing he cared about baseball was that they'd bring a beer and some peanuts to you right in your seat. No one trained me. No one told me anything."

Josh's father nodded, and he looked over at Josh as if Josh should know exactly where this was all leading.

"You know what I mean?" his father asked.

"Kind of," Josh said, not wanting to sound completely stupid but having no idea.

"Yeah," his father said, returning his attention to the road and getting off the highway and onto a boulevard lined with offices, shopping centers, and chain restaurants. "Look at that."

Up the boulevard and off to the right, back near the highway, stood an enormous white bubble that looked like a snow-covered hill.

"Used to be an indoor tennis place," his father said, pulling in and taking the long driveway that cut between a Sam's Club and Raymour's Furniture. "They went belly-up three years ago. That's when Rocky Valentine took over. You heard of Rocky? Your friends talk about him? His team?"

"I think, maybe," Josh said, "I heard someone mention his name and the Titans or something."

"Yeah," his father said, tossing him a quick glance. "Guy's amazing. Three years and he's got one of the premier youth baseball teams in the entire country. I'd heard his name but had no idea how good he really was. Did you know they won the East Cobb tournament down in Atlanta last year?"

"Wow," Josh said, doing his best to sound knowledgeable, "no."

"And this year, he says, the Titans' goal is to get to the Junior Olympics Tournament down in Fort Myers," his father said. "And if Rocky says it's their goal, you better believe they'll get there."

"Great," Josh said.

As the giant bubble came closer into view, Josh read the sign that said "Mount Olympus Sports." He knew from English class that Mount Olympus was the place where all the Greek gods lived and where the word *Olympics* came from. Titans were half men, half gods, and Josh wondered if Rocky had a reason for all the Greek references.

They came to a stop in front of the facility, pulling up behind a shiny black Porsche. The license plate said DOIT2IT.

"Guy's a businessman, too," Josh's father said, nodding at the expensive car. "He's got a DVD out hosted by

Bruce Jenner on how to make money. Owns two vitamin stores, a travel agency, a car wash, and a nightclub.

"Guy's a good guy, too," his father said. "The minute he heard about them letting me go, he's on the phone, asking me if I want to be his VP of sales."

"What do you sell?" Josh asked.

"I don't know," his father said with a shrug. "Memberships. Supplements. DVDs. Time-shares. He's into everything."

"Oh," Josh said.

His father got out and said, "Come on. Bring your glove. Wait till you see this."

Josh clutched his glove and followed his dad in through the double glass doors and past an empty reception desk. They passed by locker rooms on either side, one for men and one where the letters spelling "women" had been stripped away, leaving a clean outline in the grain of the blond wood. His father swung open one of two wide wooden doors in front of them, and they stepped out onto a concrete gallery with small metal bench seats rising up on either side and, out in front of them, an ocean of green plastic grass under a sky of black wires and stained white canvas.

Rocky, a muscular man with tan, oily skin, a black flattop haircut, and a stubble beard like Josh's dad, stood in loose red sweatpants and a skintight black T-shirt. He had folded his massive arms across his barrel chest; and while his team ran through agilities from one side of the field to the other, Rocky blasted them with his whistle. Josh and his father watched for twenty minutes while the team went from agilities to push-ups, rotating in sequences of sit-ups, up-downs, and leg raises.

"They're big," Josh said.

"It's an under-fourteen team, so most of them are ninth graders," his dad said.

"I meant big muscles, too," Josh said.

"There's a fitness center here. They come right from school every day and spend the first hour in the weight room," his father said, wearing a painful smile. "Something I never did, never knew about."

After another couple minutes, Josh quietly asked, "Do they play baseball?"

"Oh yeah," his father said. "They play. Come on."

Josh followed his father down the concrete steps and out onto the field. Rocky twittered his whistle, cutting short a set of push-ups and bringing his team in to a perfectly formed semicircle, the players sweating and gasping for air but keeping their heads held high even though they all got down on one knee.

"Gentlemen," Rocky said, his voice raspy and his words guttural, as if they could barely make their way out of that massive chest, "we have with us now Mr. Gary LeBlanc. If you're a baseball fan of any kind, and I know you guys are, you don't need me to tell you that he's the star player for the Chiefs—twelve years as a pro and a first-round draft pick right out of high school."

Rocky unfolded his arm and extended his palm toward Josh's father in a dramatic gesture. The team burst into applause.

"Gentlemen, I know Mr. LeBlanc from doing my nutritional consulting with the Chiefs, and he and I are going into a joint business venture; but what you guys will be interested to know is that his son, Josh here, is going to see if he's got what it takes to join this team."

Rocky turned to Josh and held out a meaty hand. Josh took it and winced under the crushing grip.

"Now," Rocky said, turning back to his squad, "you guys do the right thing and make Josh feel welcome. We'll see how he does, and we'll see if he can help us do it to it and get to Fort Myers."

Josh had no idea why, but he could tell by the looks on the players' faces that no matter what their coach said, every single one of them wanted to kill him.

CHAPTER TEN

JOSH KEPT UP WITH the others. He fielded the ball as well as anyone, scooping grounders, snagging pop flies, and snatching line drives like a frog snaps up gnats. His arm wasn't the strongest of the bunch, but it wasn't the weakest. Still, this bothered him, because a shortstop needs a cannon for an arm. The shortstop gets more action in the infield than anyone else. He has more ground to cover. That meant trickier glove work, and he had to make the throw to first base automatic.

The other challenge for Josh was the distance between bases. For twelve-year-old teams, the bases stood just sixty feet apart. The fourteen-year-old players competed on an adult field—ninety feet between bases—a much more difficult throw. Rocky had three younger assistant coaches, each a former collegiate player. As a group they were silent and tough. They all cut their hair close, like Rocky, and they all knew the game.

By the time they got to batting practice, Josh had a sweat going, and his arms felt heavy. He waited outside the netting, watching one of the young coaches feed yellow rubber balls into a machine throwing seventy-mile-per-hour pitches. Each player got twenty swings, and the coach tallied the hits, duffs, and strikes. Matt Jones, the tall, red-headed boy in front of Josh, connected with just seven pitches, three of them dribblers. By the time he left the cage, Jones's eyes glistened with tears.

"That's all right, Jonesy," a husky outfielder named Tucker said, patting him on the back. "This kid ain't gonna do any better than that."

Josh glanced back and saw them looking at him and understood he was the one they were talking about. He ducked through the seam in the netting and picked a bat out of the rack.

"I'll put a couple past you," the young coach named Moose said, "just so you get a feel for it. You probably haven't hit off a machine this fast before."

"That's okay," Josh said softly, stepping up to bat lefty. "I'm ready."

"Thought you were a righty," Moose said.

"My dad makes me bat both ways," Josh said.

The young coach smirked at him and muttered something as he nodded his head.

Josh clenched the bat in his hands and hefted it, letting it swing back and forth enough times to become part of him. When he stepped up to the plate, the coach fired the first pitch before Josh even had the bat back. Josh tried to swing; the pitch hit the neck of the bat, right near his hands, jarring his bones and stinging his fingers.

"Ow!" Josh cried, dropping the bat to the ground. His face burned like a spaceship plowing into the earth's atmosphere.

"Oh," the coach said with a mean smile, "I thought you were ready. Sure you don't want to bat righty?"

Josh said nothing. He bent down and gripped the bat, this time staying back for a minute to readjust. When he stepped to the plate again, the coach fired the ball. The ball came right at him. He jumped back to avoid the pitch. The kids behind him snickered, and the coach held back a smile.

"Thing throws wild sometimes," the coach said.

"That's okay," Josh said. "I saw it with Jones."

He stepped up for a third time and the ball came fast, right down the middle. Josh swung, and the metal bat clanged like a bell. The line drive nearly took off the coach's head.

"Not bad," the coach said, feeding another ball into the machine.

Josh connected again, seeing the ball the instant it left the machine, knowing where he had to swing, and choosing the way he'd hit the pitch based on its height. Anything in the lower part of the strike zone he'd chop down on, driving grounders or line drives to either side of the coach. If it came higher, he'd swing through it, blasting the ball on a trajectory that he imagined would take it into an outfield hole, if not over the fence itself.

Halfway through, Rocky reappeared and stood, arms crossed, watching Josh hit a couple from one side of the plate before stepping around to bat righty.

After the last pitch, Rocky asked, "How many?"

"All forty," the younger coach said.

"Good," Rocky said. "We'll see how he does tomorrow after lifting weights for an hour."

Rocky walked away. Josh slipped out through the seam in the netting, and the next boy stepped in. Up in the stands, Josh's father gave him a thumbs-up. Other parents sat scattered in the stands, too. Josh waved at his father and jogged off to the next batting station, where another assistant coach tossed balls up for him to hit into a net.

Ten minutes later, Rocky lined up the team along one side of the field for sprints. Josh took off on the first one, winning it and drawing glares from the kids around him. He put his head down and kept running, winning the next one as well.

"Why don't you let up, show-off," the kid next to him snarled. "We all know you came in here fresh as a daisy. Save it for tomorrow when you lift with the rest of us.

41

We'll see how fast you are then."

Josh opened his mouth to say something but thought better of it. The whistle blew again, and he took off, this time letting a handful of the older kids beat him to the line.

Finally, Rocky blew his whistle three times, signaling for the team to join him in the middle of the field. Josh took his place in the half circle and went down on one knee, huffing, his side aching and his stomach wanting to heave.

"Not a bad day today," Rocky said grudgingly. "Get your sleep and don't forget your supplements with dinner. You need to replace those amino acids. From what I've seen tonight from Josh, we may have a little competition on our hands, and that's a good thing. By the way, Josh, I need to see you and your dad in my office before you leave."

Josh caught the dirty looks other players flashed his way.

"Remember," Rocky continued, gazing around with small, dark eyes and veins bulging in his thick neck, "T-E-A-M. There's no I in team. If you're not good enough, it's not fair for you to drag down the others. Now, bring it in."

The group of boys converged on Rocky with their hands all reaching up for his, all touching one another's.

"'Do it to it,' on three!" Rocky said. "One, two, three."

"'DO IT TO IT!'" they all shouted.

The cluster broke up, and the kids started ambling toward the stands where their parents waited.

Josh touched Jones on the shoulder and in a quiet voice asked, "Jones, did I do something wrong?"

Jones flinched when Josh touched him but kept walking. Without looking back, Jones said, "Yeah, you showed up."

"What do you mean?" Josh asked, jogging to stay even with the older boy.

Jones stopped in his tracks. He glanced back at the coaches before he said in a low, snarling tone, "You think you just *join* this team? You get *chosen*. But you stumble? You're gone. Rocky finds someone better? You're gone. Some snot-nose kid with a daddy from the pros shows up to stay? It means one of us goes."

Jones turned and started to walk away.

"But don't worry," he said over his shoulder, sneering. "If us guys have anything to do with it, you'll be gone before that happens."

CHAPTER ELEVEN

ROCKY'S OFFICE OVERLOOKED THE green plastic field. Rocky's desk, like the Chiefs' GM's, faced in, toward the two chairs in which Josh and his father sat. The shelves on one wall bowed under the weight of trophies and ribbons. Several photos with ribbons strung around their frames showed Rocky atop podiums and flanked by other bodybuilders. Josh looked at the coach behind the desk, the swell of his neck and biceps. He was huge, but nothing like the man in the framed photos, who looked as if he'd stepped out of the pages of a comic book, so disproportionately large were his muscles.

"A lot of metal," Rocky said, noticing the direction of Josh's stare, "but that wall's the one I really like. My Wall of Fame."

Josh turned his attention to the opposite wall and

the pictures lined up neatly in three rows from one end to the other. In them, Josh recognized Rocky standing with his arm around various celebrities: Jessica Simpson, George Bush, AROD, LeBron James, and Al Gore.

"Wow," Josh said.

"And the secret to it all," Rocky said, pointing toward the wall behind them, where the door was, "is that stuff, Super Stax. That's how you do it to it."

Josh twisted his head around and looked back at the stacks of quart-sized cans he'd noticed when he'd walked in.

"It got me big," Rocky said, pointing toward the trophies and then to the Wall of Fame, "then it got me rich."

Rocky looked from Josh's father back to him and said, "But when you've got money and success, then you want to share it, and that's what I love to do more than anything. Your dad? A talent. I knew it the first time I saw him play. Intensity, that's what he's got. It reminded me of myself. And now you."

Rocky opened a drawer in his desk, took out a can of Super Stax, and thumped it down on the gleaming mahogany surface.

"This stuff will get you everything you've always dreamed of," Rocky said, staring hard at Josh. "It's good and it's clean. Nothing in it that isn't found in nature, and it gives you the edge you need to train harder and get bigger and stronger and faster. This first one's on me."

Rocky pushed the can across his desk at Josh. Under the name it said: NEW IMPROVED BANANA FLAVOR. Josh looked at his father, who beamed and nodded for him to go ahead.

"It's that simple," Rocky said, standing up and turning toward the field below. "Five teaspoons of this powder in a glass of milk and you're on your way. I saw your skills. You've got the raw materials. Now, if you follow me, we'll do it to it."

Rocky spun on them and extended a meaty hand.

"Deal?" he asked.

Josh let Rocky swallow his hand in an iron grip and did his best to keep his bones from crumbling as he shook. Josh's dad clasped the coach's hand, too, and they shook, grinning at each other.

Josh's dad—normally gruff and quiet—bubbled like a giddy child on the way home.

"I saw you hit," he said. "You were great. You reminded me of me. Better. I couldn't hit like that. You're twelve, but you're big enough and good enough to play with kids two years older, and those kids are the best around. This is going to work, Josh. I *know* it is. It's what I needed."

His father looked over at him, and his face grew serious. "It's what I never had."

Josh sat quietly for a minute before he said, "They said it won't be so easy after lifting weights for an hour. I don't know about the weights thing. I never did that."

His father waved a hand in the air as they pulled off the highway and turned up the hill into their north-side neighborhood.

"I talked to Rocky about that," he said. "People used to think kids shouldn't lift until fourteen or fifteen; but all the experts are saying now that kids can start a lot earlier, especially with Super Stax. Josh, if I had what you're going to get—this kind of training—who knows how far I could have gone? I guarantee I would have been in the Majors. You don't realize it because you're so much better than the kids you play with, but that's the problem. You get out into the real world—the real world of baseball—and you realize you can't just be good. You have to be great."

Josh said nothing until they pulled into their garage.

"I'd rather play with my friends, Dad," he said.

His father shut off the car and stared at him. The engine ticked, and his father's breathing filled the car. Finally, he said, "You have no idea, Josh. You think friends are important? You want to be a pro player, don't you?"

Josh nodded.

"In the big leagues?"

"Yes."

Josh's dad gripped a handful of his son's shirt and pulled Josh close.

"Then you'll do what I tell you," his father said in a tense whisper. "What happened to me isn't going to happen to you. If I had someone like Rocky, I'd be in Toronto right now. No, I would have been in New York with the Mets. I didn't have the strength. I had all the talent but none of the training."

Josh watched his father's eyes, the yellow rings expanding and contracting around the deep brown irises that made Josh think of the black holes in space, holes so dense and full of mass that they suck in everything—light, planets, even suns and stars—from light-years away. For a moment Josh didn't recognize his father, so distant were those eyes. A shiver ran down his spine, and he realized his father was waiting for him to reply.

CHAPTER TWELVE

"OKAY," JOSH SAID.

"Good," his father said, releasing him and getting out of the car.

Josh followed his father out the garage door, across the driveway, and into the kitchen. The smell of beef stew greeted them along with the smiling faces of both Benji and, to Josh's surprise, Jaden Neidermeyer. Josh's mom had set out two extra places at the small kitchen table, putting him between Jaden and Benji. Benji ate dinner with them often. Since Josh's best friend lived alone with his mom and she worked most evenings, Benji had his own place at their kitchen table. Jaden, on the other hand, hadn't even met Josh's mom until twenty minutes ago.

"Your friends were worried about you," his mom

49

explained as she bent over the high chair to put a bib on Josh's little sister, Laurel. "Benji's staying for dinner, so I invited Jaden, too. Benji, fill the glasses for me, will you?"

Josh's father said hello to their guests, then plunked the Super Stax down on the counter.

"Make sure you get five tablespoons into your milk," he said to Josh before disappearing to wash his hands. Josh washed his own hands in the kitchen sink before stirring the Super Stax into his milk glass. Jaden watched him, and he eyed her suspiciously. He'd seen her around plenty in school but had never really spoken to her until yesterday.

The pace of her involvement in his life was disconcerting. First she writes the glowing article about him in the school paper, then she sits with him at lunch, and the next thing he knows, she's having dinner with his family. Benji wagged his eyebrows at Josh as he poured the milk. Josh answered Benji's smirk with a dirty look. He could imagine what Benji was thinking: At this rate Josh would be married to her by next week.

Jaden sat with her hands and napkin in her lap, her back straight, and her wild, frizzy hair pulled back with a wide green ribbon.

"I came to do a follow-up story," she said to Josh, picking up the notebook underneath her leg, showing it to him, then replacing it, "and your mom asked me if I like beef stew."

Josh sat down and shot his mom a glance. She had her back to them, working over a steaming cauldron on the stove, then draining off a pot of noodles in the sink. His father walked back into the kitchen, kissed Laurel on the cheek, and studied Josh's face, waiting for him to answer Jaden.

Josh knew—after years of having dinner guests of all kinds—better than to be impolite. He'd find himself grounded for a week if he did anything to make Jaden feel unwelcome.

"Great," Josh said, sitting down beside her with his milk. "My mom makes the best."

Josh put the glass to his lips and swallowed tentatively. His milk tasted like rotten bananas and cough medicine. Josh made a sour face.

"What's wrong?" his father said, scowling.

"Nothing," Josh said, forcing a smile onto his face, holding his breath, and gulping down his milk.

"Did you know Jaden's dad is a doctor at the hospital?" Josh's mom asked as she set a bowl of stew down on the table along with a bowl of noodles. "He works all kinds of crazy hours."

"Wow," Josh said.

"He's a resident physician," Jaden said, beaming proudly.

Her southern accent seemed more subdued than it had when she spoke in the cafeteria, and Josh wondered if it got more pronounced when she was nervous.

"When he's done," Jaden said, "he'll be an orthopedic surgeon. Hopefully, he'll work for the Yankees."

Benji wrinkled his nose and said, "Yankees? I thought you were from South Carolina."

"Texas," Jaden said, slipping into the drawl, "but my father grew up in New York, and we're Yankees fans."

"Dude," Benji said, "they stink."

"You might say that if you're a fan of the Red Sox or one of the other lesser teams," Jaden said calmly, "but then you'd be denying the dominance of the franchise throughout the history of baseball."

Benji made choking noises until Josh's dad cast him a dark look.

"Sorry, Mr. LeBlanc," Benji said, sitting up straight and folding his hands. "Would you like me to say grace?"

Josh rolled his eyes. Benji's clowning sometimes got him into trouble, but he always knew how to kiss up to the adults.

After grace, they dug into the stew, and Josh's dad asked, "Jaden, I heard you say you were here for a story. Josh's mom told me about the nice article you wrote about him in the school paper. What are you working on now?"

Jaden finished her mouthful, took a small swallow of milk, and dabbed her lips with the napkin from her lap. She looked unflinchingly at Josh's dad and said, "The story about why he's not going to play for the team, Mr.

LeBlanc. It's big news, for Grant Middle, anyway. You should have seen Coach Miller's face after you left."

"I thought he was going to *cry*," Benji said just as a belch escaped his lips. "Excuse me."

"Jeez," Josh said, rolling his eyes and, for some reason, feeling embarrassed.

"What?" Benji said. "In Mongolia, when you burp it's like telling the cook the food's great, and I love your mom's stew. You are such a good cook, Mrs. LeBlanc."

"You're so sweet, Benji," Josh's mom said.

"Good grief," Josh said.

"Josh has an opportunity to play on one of the best U14 travel teams in the country," Josh's father said to Jaden.

"What team?" Jaden asked, taking her notebook back out from under her leg and unclipping its pen.

Josh's dad glanced at the notebook, then slowly said, "Rocky Valentine's team, the Mount Olympus Titans."

Jaden curled her lower lip up under her teeth, then quietly asked, "Mr. LeBlanc, wasn't he the guy whose team got asked to leave the U13 tournament in Dayton last summer? I remember Bud Poliquin wrote about it in the *Post-Standard*."

Josh's dad snorted and shook his head, forcing a smile onto his face. "I have no idea what you're talking about."

"It was all kind of weird," Jaden said, her excitement growing. "No one from the tournament would say why. All the parents were mad. Rocky Valentine never said anything to anyone, and the whole thing just went away."

"Right, the whole thing went away," Josh's father said, keeping his voice pleasant but wearing a look on his face that made Josh shift in his seat. "So, why are you bringing it back up?"

CHAPTER THIRTEEN

JADEN LOOKED AT JOSH'S father's face for a moment, and her lip disappeared into her teeth again. She replaced the pen and tucked the notebook back under her leg.

"I'm sorry," she said. "My dad says a good reporter asks the questions other people want to know but are afraid to ask. This stew *is* great, Mrs. LeBlanc."

"If you like it as much as I do," Benji said, "let one fly."

Laurel burped and banged her spoon on the tray attached to her chair, giggling.

"There you go," Benji said with a grin and a nod.

"Save it for Mongolia," Josh's father said, his low voice rumbling.

"Sorry, Mr. LeBlanc," Benji said, dropping his voice and his chin to his chest.

They ate the rest of the meal in relative silence. Josh's mom did her best to spark conversation about the new hotel that was supposed to go up next to the Destiny USA shopping mall beside the lake, but no one picked up the slack. When he finished, Josh's father excused himself, telling Josh's mother that he had some work to do.

"It was nice to meet you, Jaden," he said pleasantly, stopping in the doorway. "I hope you'll come again."

"Thank you," Jaden said, and smiled up at him.

"Josh," his mother said after watching his father disappear, "I'll clean up. Why don't you and Benji walk Jaden to the hospital? She has to meet her father there at eight."

"Why?" Josh asked, but caught his mom's icy glare and immediately changed his tone. "Sure. Yeah. That'd be great."

"That's okay, Mrs. LeBlanc," Jaden said, getting up and taking some plates to the sink. "I'll help you and then I can take myself. I walk by myself all the time. We live right on the corner of Pond and Carbon, so it's not far."

"You're sweet," Josh's mom said, "but I wouldn't feel comfortable if Josh didn't walk you. I asked you to stay and I want to make sure you get there okay. Josh and Benji can use the exercise anyway."

Josh wanted to tell his mom that his limbs felt like jelly and exercise was the last thing he needed, but he knew better all the way around. Besides, for whatever reason, what Jaden said to his dad had struck a nerve, and Josh knew once his dad's nerves got struck, you were better off letting things settle down. He took his own dishes to the sink and got his coat.

Outside, Benji started in on Jaden immediately.

"Nice going," Benji said. "The guy has his life destroyed, and you're pumping him about Rocky Valentine."

"Destroyed?" Jaden said.

"It's not *destroyed*," Josh said, scowling at Benji as they turned from the driveway onto the sidewalk.

"Crushed?" Benji asked with a shrug.

"He's fine," Josh said. "Rocky Valentine offered him a job."

"Wait a minute," Jaden said, stopping in her tracks. "What are you two talking about?"

"His dad got cut, dude," Benji said.

"He kind of retired," Josh said.

"He's the best player on that team," Jaden said. "His batting average is three twenty-one."

Josh wrinkled his face, started walking, and said, "Do you have to know everything?"

Jaden caught up and raised her eyebrows. "I'm just saying."

"'Cause it's annoying," Benji said, hustling up beside them. "What do you have, like, a photographic memory? Why do you even bother with that stupid pad?"

"I don't know," Jaden said.

"Right," Josh said. "I believe that."

"So," she said, ignoring him, "your dad's not playing anymore and he's going to work for Rocky Valentine? What's he doing?"

"Some kind of VP," Josh said under his breath, "like sales or something."

"And what was that stuff in your milk?" Jaden asked.

Josh shrugged. "Some supplement for working out. It's all natural. Super Stax, in case you want to Google it."

"I will," Jaden said, marching along.

"Good," Josh said.

"Great," she said.

Josh stopped suddenly and grabbed her arm.

"Do you smell that?" he asked.

"What? That smoke?" she said.

"Cigarette smoke?" Benji asked, his voice quavering.

Bart Wilson suddenly stepped out from behind the bushes, blocking their path on the sidewalk.

"Going someplace, punk?"

CHAPTER FOURTEEN

BART PITCHED HIS CIGARETTE down onto the sidewalk. It rolled, burning, to the edge of the grass, filling the air with its stench.

"That's disgusting," Jaden said.

Bart narrowed his eyes at her, then said to Josh, "Let's go, punk. You and me."

"Oh, dude," Benji said, and he took off down the sidewalk, running back the way they came, the clap of his feet sounding lonely on the empty concrete.

Josh's insides melted. He looked from Jaden to the tenth grader and shook his head.

"Get out of here," Jaden said, taking out her cell phone and beginning to dial. "Before I call the cops."

Bart swatted her hand, and the cell phone clattered to the sidewalk.

"What are you?" Bart asked with a sneer. "Some kind of African, Asian, Mexican, or something?"

"I'm a human being," Jaden said, "which is more than you can say, you disgusting animal."

Bart laughed at her.

"She's the prettiest girl in school," Josh said, swallowing.

Bart turned and studied him. "Want to fight about *that*?"

Josh balled up his hands into fists. His heart hammered the inside of his rib cage, and he thought it might explode. He slowly raised his hands.

"Get out of here!" Jaden shouted, stepping between them and putting her face just inches from Bart's, her voice strong and southern. "You stay here a second longer and I'll file a police complaint against you for harassment. You touch him or me and I'll file one for assault. You think you can just do this? You can't. My dad's a cop and he'll hunt you down and throw you in jail so fast you won't know where you are until the big boys behind bars are smacking you around and you're crying for your momma."

Bart stood there, huffing at her.

"Josh is *my* boyfriend," Jaden said suddenly in her drawl. "He doesn't want anything to do with Sheila. You can tell her that. You want to fight someone? Go fight with her, and tell her to stay away from Josh."

"That's bull crap," Bart said, snarling.

"Go ahead," Jaden said, gritting her teeth. "You just

touch me and see what happens to you. Wait till I tell my father you're a racist, too. He'll slap the cuffs on extra tight."

Bart lunged at Jaden but pulled back just before he touched her.

Jaden never flinched.

"You think I'm scared of *you*?" Jaden said, wrinkling up her face.

Bart took a step back and said, "You better be, 'cause when I get you back, you ain't gonna see me coming. There ain't gonna be no cops, and there ain't gonna be no witnesses."

Bart turned and started away before spinning around and walking backward as he spoke. "Both of you, you better watch your backs."

Bart kept going, now laughing demonically at them.

Jaden just stood staring and shaking her head. "What a moron."

When Bart rounded the corner, Josh asked, "You think he'll do it?"

"Do what?"

"Get us."

Jaden swatted the air, scooped up her cell phone, and said, "Come on. I don't want to be late for my dad. If he comes out and I'm not there, he'll walk home alone."

Josh hurried to catch up to her.

"He's not really a cop, too, is he?" Josh asked, falling in alongside her.

Jaden furrowed her brow and glanced at him,

shaking her head again.

"No," she said. "Just a doctor."

"Well, you sounded pretty good," Josh said.

"I said you were my boyfriend, too," Jaden said. "And we both know that's bologna. Even if I wanted to—which I don't—my father won't let me date until I'm sixteen."

"That's good," Josh said, his face suddenly burning. "I don't mean because of me or anything. I mean that he cares about you like that."

"Speaking of caring," Jaden said, "your buddy Benji lit out like a cockroach."

"He's a good guy," Josh said, looking over his shoulder in the direction Benji had disappeared. "He might have gone for help."

"Well, I sure didn't hear any cavalry bugles," Jaden said.

"Does your voice do that a lot?" he asked.

"Do what?"

"You talk kind of southern when you're excited," he said.

She shrugged without comment.

They walked for a block in silence before Jaden said, "Don't you know you could twist that moron up into a pretzel?"

"Who, Bart?"

"Yeah," Jaden said. "You'd kill him."

"He's a lot older than me," Josh said.

"So he's older," Jaden said. "I'm glad you don't want to fight—that's for morons. But if it came down to it, you'd kill him, and you don't even know it."

"I guess," Josh said, straightening his back a little.

"But don't worry," Jaden said. "I've seen the type. He's all talk. Here it is."

They had come to the big brick hospital that covered three city blocks. Before them stood the loading docks, a dark cavern of concrete cut into the side of the hill. Enormous garage doors stood in a row deep in the shadows beyond the raised platform, and a handful of Dumpsters had been crowded into the far corner of the blacktop below. Several cars had been nosed up along part of the concrete wall near the Dumpsters. One caught Josh's eye.

A sliver of light appeared, then grew into a rectangle from which emerged the shadow of a person.

"He always comes out the back," Jaden said, nodding toward the door.

Josh watched as a second dark figure appeared from the shadows and approached Jaden's dad.

"Who parks back here?" Josh asked, watching as the second figure melted back into the shadows as if it had never been there at all.

Jaden shrugged. Looking at Josh, she said, "People dropping things off or picking them up, I guess. Why?"

"That's a nice car," Josh said, pointing to the small black one in the middle of the others as Jaden's father jogged down the concrete steps still wearing a long white examination coat.

"That Porsche? It is nice," Jaden said. "When my dad's working for the Yankees, I'm hoping he'll get something like that."

"Yeah, I know someone who's got one of those," Josh said.

"Really? One of the Chiefs?" Jaden asked.

"Coach Valentine," Josh said, walking toward the car to get a look at the license plate in the shadows, unable to make it out. "But what would he be doing here?"

Jaden kissed her father hello and introduced him to Josh. Josh shook the doctor's hand, but his eyes were on the black car.

"Better look out," Jaden's father said. "Here comes a truck."

Together, they moved away from the center of the blacktop. As the truck pulled in, its headlights shone on the row of cars. Josh blinked and saw, without a doubt, a license plate that read DOIT2IT.

CHAPTER FIFTEEN

"I THOUGHT WE WERE all running," Benji said with all the surprise he could muster.

Josh rolled his eyes. Jaden took a bite of her sandwich without saying anything.

"What?" Benji said. "You think I was afraid? I knew you didn't want to fight that guy, and I figured if I hightailed it out of there, you'd follow. By the time I turned around, you guys were gone. I sent a text, but glamour boy here had his phone off."

"What'd you do?" Jaden said. "Run till you hit the Canadian border?"

"Now, that's the kind of thing that makes it hard to be your friend," Benji said, scolding her with his index finger.

"I'm so upset, I'm going to have to stop eating," Jaden

said, taking a huge bite of her sandwich and chewing wildly.

"Don't worry, Lido," Josh said through a mouthful of lettuce and bologna on white bread. "I know you got my back if I need you."

"Yeah, you know that, dude," Benji said with a defiant nod at Jaden.

Jaden just closed her eyes.

The rest of the school day went as well as school can go, with no pop quizzes and not a lot of homework. Josh had to dodge the other kids on the team and their questions as best he could, and to those he couldn't dodge he'd just shrug and say he couldn't do anything about it. His dad needed him.

At two-twenty, those who didn't believe him had the chance to see him run down the front steps of the school, pass the buses, and jump into his dad's waiting car, which sped all the way to the Mount Olympus Sports Complex.

When they arrived, Josh and his dad saw cars, trucks, and SUVs racing in and out of the circle in front of the giant bubble. It reminded Josh of a pit stop, with each player jumping from his parents' vehicle and sprinting for the door.

Josh's dad wished him good luck and told him he'd be back to watch the end of practice. Josh got out of the car and, caught up in the atmosphere, hurried inside like the others. He changed into workout shorts and a

T-shirt in the locker room, then followed the stream of players into the weight room.

Stacks of metal plates clapped together intermittently, making the whole place sound like a construction site. The smell of rubber mats and stale sweat filled the air, along with the grunts, shouts, and angry cries of the lifters. Josh looked around, blinking, before the young assistant named Moose took him by the arm and showed him to the counter where the workout cards waited for the players in a plastic file box.

"Here's yours," Moose said. "I filled in the weights you should use, just guessing. I'll go around with you today, show you the circuit, and we'll adjust the weights up or down depending on how you do. You ready?"

"Sure," Josh said. He looked around at the other players. None of them spoke to one another. They trudged from machine to machine with the urgency of firefighters at a blaze.

Moose showed Josh the two sides of his card, one for leg days, one for upper body.

"We split the team in half," Moose said. "You're in the upper-body group for today, so you'll do seven sets of bench presses and all the upper-body machines in between. Wednesday, we do plyometrics—jumping exercises. Thursday, you'll do legs. Friday, back to upper, then legs again on Monday. Got it?"

Josh examined the 8 x 10 lime green card and nodded.

"Here we go," Moose said, looking around the room. "You start where you can. There, biceps."

Josh wedged himself into a padded machine and gripped a scored bar.

"You go till failure, plus two," Moose said. "Today, I'll show you what that means. Tomorrow, you're on your own, and you just get anyone you can to spot you and push you past failure."

"Failure?"

"Till you can't do any more," Moose said. "Then your spotter helps you do two more beyond that, but he makes you do the work. That's how you get stronger."

Josh glanced at Jones as he pushed past the machine where Josh sat. To Moose, Josh said, "I don't know if these guys are going to want to help me."

"Oh, they'll help," Moose growled. "This is my weight room. Someone doesn't help a teammate in here and they're gone. We already lost one guy that way. Rocky won't have it, and neither will I. Go ahead, get started. I put fifty on here for you. Do as many as you can."

After the eighth repetition Josh's arms began to tremble, and he got the handles only halfway up.

"Finish!" Moose screamed, helping him just a bit as Josh struggled to bring up the bar.

"Now down slow," Moose said, pushing on the weights as Josh let the bar down.

Josh did his best to keep it from dropping, but Moose pushed it down and said, "That stinks. You gotta be tougher than that. Come on, two more now, up fast and down slow."

Josh's arms trembled and ached, and he fought to get the bar back up two more times, then hold it on the way down. By the time Moose let him off the machine, his head pounded and his brow dripped with sweat.

"Next," Moose said, pointing to a bench press. "Let's go. You only got an hour."

Moose dragged Josh through the weight room, yelling and screaming and urging him on. By the time Josh walked out, his muscles quivered like Jell-O and his arms felt heavier than lead. He returned to the locker room and slowly changed into fresh clothes, then jogged out with the others under the echoes of Rocky's blasting whistle. Agility drills and stretching wore him down even more, and he felt half a step slow in the fielding drills. His throws to first base made it, but as the session wore on, he had to put an arc on the ball to get it there.

Rocky's whistle sounded three shrill blasts in a row, and everything stopped. From behind home plate, he screamed at Josh.

"You throw like that and I got a troop of Girl Scouts who could make it safe to first base running backward!" Rocky said. "That's crap! Total crap! Make the throw or get out of there!"

Josh's eyes felt hot with tears. Jones smirked at him from his position on first, and Jones's buddy Tucker snorted with quiet laughter from behind him in right field. The drill started up again. Josh kept his head up, took the next grounder, and rifled it. He felt a sharp pain in his shoulder, but the ball smacked Jones's glove, wiping the smile off Jones's face.

"That's better!" Rocky shouted.

Josh wanted to grab his shoulder, but he forced himself not to, hoping and praying that he'd have a rest before the next grounder came his way. He did, and by the time he had to make another play, the pain had subsided to a dull ache. With the throw came the bolt of pain, but instead of flinching, Josh growled with anger. He set his teeth and ground his way through practice, letting the pain in his arm fuel his rage and his determination not to quit.

As the minutes of practice ticked by, his shoulder grew sorer and sorer. He kept on, part of him wishing time could speed up. The other part of him wanted time to stop because he knew every minute also brought him closer to hitting practice.

And Josh had no idea how he'd swing a bat.

When his turn came to enter the batting cage, Josh took a deep breath and ducked inside.

CHAPTER SIXTEEN

JONES BUMPED INTO HIM hard, striking Josh's sore shoulder and knocking him back.

"Let me get out, will you?" Jones said.

"Sorry," Josh said, sidestepping the older player and tugging on his batting gloves. He hefted a bat, but it didn't sit right in his hands. Even a slow swing sent shards of pain down his arm.

"Let's go," the young coach behind the pitching machine said. "I don't have all night here."

Josh stepped up to the plate, and the first pitch came at him like a shot; the yellow rubber baseball from the machine was a blur. He swung and missed, and the coach fired another. Josh barely had his bat back in place. He swung again and missed, his shoulder on fire. Tucker chortled from outside the net.

Josh heard Tucker say under his breath, "Thinks he can bat both sides of the plate."

Besides the pain, Josh's arms felt as they had the time he'd fallen into the deep end of his friend's pool in Manchester with his clothes on—sluggish and slow.

Another pitch came and another miss.

"Three strikes, you're out," Tucker said.

Josh saw the coach make a check on his clipboard, then feed another ball into the machine. Another whiff.

Josh stepped back and held up one hand.

"What now?" the coach asked. "You wanna change to righty?"

Josh turned to the bat rack and found the shortest bat they had. He picked it up and felt the lightness. Maybe he couldn't blast line drives and homers, but he'd be darned if he'd let any more pitches by him. His shoulder might hurt and his arms might be exhausted, but he could still see the ball and read its path.

He gritted his teeth, swung the new bat three times, and stepped up to the plate, still as a lefty. He narrowed his eyes and focused on the tube that launched the balls.

The pitch came.

He swung, more with his wrists than his arms.

Crack.

A grounder through the hole between first and second. The next pitch came. *Crack.* Another grounder.

Another pitch. *Crack*. Another. *Crack*.

Josh missed only two of the remaining sixteen swings as a lefty, then hit every one from the other side of the plate. None of the hits had any power, but Josh knew the coach couldn't do anything but mark them down as hits. He went to his next station, then joined the entire team for sprints before Rocky called them in.

"A crap practice today," Rocky said, glowering. "You want to do it to it? You gotta work harder than this. I don't have anything else to say other than if you do this to me tomorrow, you better tell your mommies and daddies to find you girls a new coach."

Rocky turned abruptly and stormed off the field.

"Okay," Moose said, picking up the slack and raising a hand that the rest of them rallied around. "'Do it to it' on three. One, two, three."

"DO IT TO IT!"

Josh dragged himself back to the locker room, arriving last. The other players dug into their lockers, pulling out gym bags, some of them changing into dry clothes. At first, Josh attributed the quiet to Rocky chewing them out, but when he reached into his gym bag, he recoiled.

"Yuck!" he said.

The rest of the players burst into laughter and applause.

Josh looked around at their laughing faces and then

down at the slippery goo all over his hands and inside his bag.

From the back, someone shouted, "We figured you could use it, to butter up the coach!"

Josh looked at the yellow mess, half of him ashamed and angry, the other half glad that it was only butter.

"Or save it for yourself, since you're gonna be toast!"

Josh looked for the source of the voice, a stubby kid named Perkins, the team's backup second baseman. Perkins stared at Josh from beneath an eave of blunt-cut blond bangs and grinned with a set of buckteeth that many kids would be ashamed of. Without thinking, Josh walked over to Perkins and stood toe-to-toe, looking down.

"What are you gonna do, you little twelve-year-old sissy?" Perkins snarled. "Butter me up, too?"

Jaden—and Bart Wilson—flashed across Josh's mind, and without thinking, Josh grabbed a handful of Perkins's T-shirt and slammed him into the lockers with a crash.

"Fight. Fight. Fight," the others chanted.

Perkins's eyes went wide. He staggered sideways, slapping Josh's hands off him. Perkins snarled and charged with his head down. Josh sidestepped Perkins, grabbed the back of his collar in one hand and the waist of his pants in the other, and hurled Perkins like a battering ram into the opposite lockers.

The lockers shook under the bang, and Perkins crumpled to his knees, pawing at his bloody head.

The locker-room door thundered open.

"What the heck is going on in here!"

Josh whirled and stared into the sweaty purple face of Rocky Valentine.

CHAPTER SEVENTEEN

"NOTHING, COACH," JONES SAID, stepping in front of the fallen Perkins. "We're just fooling around."

"Fooling around?" Rocky said, glaring at Josh. "LeBlanc, you fooling around?"

Josh opened his mouth, but nothing came out.

"Well?" Rocky said.

Josh nodded his head. "A little, Coach."

"You think that's what we do around here?" Rocky asked, his jaw snapping as he worked it back and forth.

"No, Coach," Josh said.

"Do you?" Rocky asked Jones.

"No, Coach."

"Perkins," Rocky said, looking around Jones. "Get up and get out of here. I don't want to see any of you anymore. Go on! Get out!"

Josh grabbed his bag and scrambled out of the locker room with the rest of them. His dad met him with a somber face in the lobby, put an arm around his shoulder, and guided him outside toward their car. Josh climbed in and tucked the slimy bag under his legs.

When they were under way, Josh's father said, "That was some pretty weak batting in the cage."

Josh rubbed his shoulder. "I never lifted weights before."

"Well, you'll get used to it," his father said. "That's part of it. You gotta toughen up a little bit. That's one thing for me with having two older brothers—I didn't need to toughen up. They did it for me."

Josh's father grinned at him.

"How's the job going?" Josh asked.

"Not bad," his father said. "Getting into it a little. Rocky wants to start expanding his baseball teams—you know, a U12 and a U16—so I'll get involved with that a little. Sell it a little. Get some coaches lined up, some players, maybe. Do it to it. We've got the Super Stax franchise for the area, so I'm starting to set up meetings with the different coaches and trainers at the universities around here."

Josh let that sink in before he said, "And that stuff's good, right?"

"What? Super Stax?"

Josh nodded.

"You think I'd have you taking it if it wasn't?" his father said. "It's proven. If you don't like the banana, they got it in chocolate, too."

"No, banana's okay."

"Josh," his father said, stopping at a red light and looking over at him. "I know it's hard, but it gets easier. Trust me. Your body will adjust. Especially with the Super Stax. That's what it's for, to build muscle."

Telling his father about Rocky's car at the hospital danced on the tip of Josh's tongue, but the direction of the conversation made him certain it would sound stupid, so he dropped it. After a few minutes, he turned the radio on to fill the silence while he replayed the fight with Perkins in his mind. Before today, Josh had never been in a fight.

When they got home, Josh choked down a glass of milk with Super Stax, then gobbled down two plates of his mom's spaghetti and meatballs. He tried to play a game of Candy Land with Laurel while his mom cleaned up the kitchen, but Laurel kept chewing the cards. After that he polished off what little homework he had, kissed his parents good-night, and crawled into bed early with a copy of *Heat*. He only got through a couple chapters before his eyes grew heavy, and he fell asleep without bothering to turn off the light.

Josh woke, and panic raced through his veins. His left leg wouldn't move. He rolled from the bed and hit the floor, the feeling returning in the form of a million needles. Every other muscle in his body shrieked with pain. Josh groaned and pawed at the bed to help himself rise. He limped down the narrow hall to the bathroom. His father was just coming out, wearing only the bottoms of his red and white striped pajamas. His father's hair was a mess and his beard extra stubbly.

"Dad," Josh moaned. "I'm sore all over. I can barely move. My shoulder."

Josh clutched his aching right arm.

His father studied him for a few seconds with his lips pressed tight before he said, "Hang on. I got something to help you."

His father ducked back into the bathroom, and Josh followed him. His father opened the medicine cabinet behind the mirror and jiggled some pills out of a prescription bottle.

"Here," his father said, handing Josh a little octagonal yellow pill.

Josh turned the pill over in his fingers and asked, "What is it?"

"Anti-inflammatory," his father said. "Go ahead. It'll help."

"Can I?" Josh asked. "You don't have to check with the doctor or anything?"

His father frowned and made an impatient gesture with his hand. "You think I don't know about this stuff?"

"No." Josh said. "I mean, yes. I know you know."

"You'll feel better," his dad said, pushing past him and shuffling off toward his bedroom. "Medicine is part of sports. The higher you go, the more you have to get used to that. It's just part of the game. Don't worry. It's safe."

Josh looked at the pill and the tiny numbers stamped on its face. He filled a paper cup with water and washed down the pill, then looked at himself in the mirror to see if anything had changed.

CHAPTER EIGHTEEN

JADEN STARTED SITTING WITH Josh and Benji at lunch every day. Bart Wilson didn't show his face around the neighborhood, and Sheila made a point of walking past Josh in the halls, just so she could turn up her nose. The second article Jaden wrote about Josh in the school's weekly paper didn't take up much space. It explained the situation with him joining the Titans in a sympathetic light and pointed out that with Kerry Eschelman's arm, the team should be a contender anyway.

The Mount Olympus Titans continued their grueling practice sessions, but the excruciating soreness Josh felt in the mornings began to ease up. He stopped taking the little yellow pills and learned to pack his throwing arm in ice every night before bed.

Josh, Jaden, and Benji teamed up for a science poster

project that brought them all together at Josh's house on a Thursday evening. Josh's mom made a stir-fry of chicken and vegetables that everyone loved before the three partners spread out their materials on the living-room floor.

"Benji," Jaden asked, "what are you doing?"

Benji sat with his back against the wall, and he looked up from his notebook only after writing something down. His face turned red and he said, "Just a little math."

"We're doing science," Jaden said. "Our *team* project?"

"I just figured, while you guys were working out the details, I could get this done," Benji said. "I'm not a good detail guy. I'm more of the big-picture type."

Jaden looked at Josh, appealing for help.

"Come on, man," Josh said. "We gotta work together."

"Well, I'm a science genius, but this math stuff is killing me," Benji said, rumpling up his face. "I got a sixty-four right now and if I fail, I'm off the baseball team. I know that doesn't mean much to a big travel team star like you, but us little people got to eat, too."

Jaden scooted over next to him and examined his notebook.

"Where's your work on this problem?" she asked.

Benji shrugged. "What do you mean?"

"Your work," she said. "The calculations for the problem. You've got the formula right, but the answer's wrong. Where did you do the work?"

Benji crunched his eyebrows and said, "I sit right next to you in math. I see the way you do it, and you've got, what? A hundred and two average?"

Jaden looked at him, and her face relaxed. She shook her head and softly said, "I think if you just do the work out on paper, you'll be fine. There's a lot of calculations you have to make with this. If you write it down, it's ten times easier to keep track of. Here, let me show you."

Benji watched her, nodding his head.

"Yeah, I get that, dude," he said. "Just what I was doing, but in my head."

"So," Jaden said patiently, "if you just write it down like this, I think you'll be golden. The formula is the hardest part, and you got that."

"Yeah," Benji said, "that I got. That's the hard part. But I still don't get why I shouldn't do it the same way as you."

"She's smarter than you, meathead," Josh said. "Don't get mad. She's smarter than me, too."

"But she can't swing a bat like me," Benji said, grinning.

"That's why you're her hero," Josh said. "Now that you've solved the meaning of life, can we get back to this poster? I got to get to bed."

Benji wrinkled his brow and said, "Anyone else tell you this Titans baseball team has turned you into a real bore?"

"Tomorrow, I'm either in or out," Josh said, "so you might not have to worry about it."

"What's tomorrow?" Jaden asked.

"We got a tournament down on Long Island this weekend," Josh said. "Rocky says the team has to be down to eighteen, so somebody's got to go."

"Not you!" Jaden asked.

"I'm the only twelve-year-old."

"So what," Jaden said. "I can't believe you're not as good as any fourteen-year-old. You're as big as most of them, right?"

"Kind of."

"So?" Jaden said.

"I'm not the strongest," he said. "Not even close."

"You don't have to be the strongest to hit," Jaden said. "Or play shortstop."

"It helps," Josh said. "But I'm getting better."

"That stuff you drink at dinner when you hold your nose?" Jaden asked.

"You ever check out what that stuff is?" Benji asked her.

"The technical name is arginine alpha-ketoglutarate," she said. "In theory, it replenishes the nitrogen in your cells and enhances the production of amino acids, the building blocks for muscle development."

"What?" Benji said, his eyes wide. "Steroids?"

CHAPTER NINETEEN

"NO," JADEN AND JOSH said at the same time.

Josh looked at her, and she said to Benji, "A supplement. Like food. Some people don't even think they do anything. There've been studies that show placebos to be just as effective."

"What's a placebo?" Benji asked.

Jaden sighed and said, "They tell people they're getting a supplement, but they just give them sugar pills with nothing in them. In some tests it works just as well. People think they're going to get stronger, and they do."

"Maybe I should be using that Stax stuff," Benji said.

"They probably just work harder," Jaden said. "Now, can we do this poster?"

"Bite my head off," Benji said.

"Well, first we're doing a math tutorial," Jaden said, "and now we're doing the ESPN *Sports Reporters*."

"I'm a man of many interests and many talents," Benji said, placing a hand over his heart. "That's how you get *personality*."

"Last I checked, that wasn't a college major," Jaden said, picking up a chart and beginning to snip away the edges with a pair of scissors.

"Major?" Benji said. "I'm majoring in baseball— that's if I don't go straight to the pros."

"Then how come you're not the one with the Titans?" Jaden asked, coating the back of the chart with a glue stick.

"When I'm developed, that's all," Benji said. "So I'm not a behemoth like my buddy here. I'll grow, and when I do, I'll be right there next to him, leading off."

"I won't be there myself if we don't get this done and I get some sleep," Josh said.

They got to work, and at 9:07, Josh's friends walked out together. He got ready for bed and went down into the TV room to kiss his parents good-night. His mom worked on a Sudoku puzzle from the couch while his dad sat stretched back in his recliner, watching a Yankees game.

"Bed already?" his mom asked.

"We find out tomorrow who gets cut," Josh said. He watched his dad but got no reaction until cheers came from the TV.

"You see that double play?" his father asked.

Josh turned and watched the replay.

"That'll be you," his dad said.

"So, you think I'll make it?" Josh asked.

His dad clicked the remote, muting the TV, and said, "I don't know, Josh."

"You're kidding, right?" Josh said. "I mean, you work with Rocky, right?"

His father shook his head and said, "It doesn't work that way. Rocky's not going to keep you unless he and his coaches think you're better than someone else. You probably have to be a lot better than the older kids for them to keep you, Josh."

Josh felt pressure build up in his face, and before he could stop himself he shouted, "Then why did I do all this?"

Josh's mother put aside her puzzle and glanced nervously between Josh and his father. Josh's father reached down and cranked on the lever of his chair, bringing it upright and sitting tall.

"You did it to be the best," his father said. "You did it because if you make this team, you're on your way. If you make it, everyone will be talking about you. Twelve-year-olds just can't play with fourteen-year-olds, everyone knows that."

"You didn't!" Josh said.

His father stared at him for a minute, then in a low, tight voice said, "I knew exactly what I was doing. I wanted to see if you've got what it takes, not just hitting and fielding, but mentally, see if you're tough enough to make it. Part of that is facing facts. If you're good enough, you'll make the cut. If you're not, then you go back to the drawing board and start over."

"But I can't go back to the drawing board, Dad," Josh said, his voice still raised. "I quit the school team, and I can't go back now. They made their cuts."

His father flicked his hand and said, "School team. That's crap. Mount Olympus is going to have a U12 travel team put together in a week or so. We got Dickie Woodridge lined up as batting coach, and if it goes good with the Nike people, Rocky might even let me manage the whole thing, so you can play there."

Josh thought about Benji and Esch and the other kids he had looked forward to becoming friends with by playing together, being the team's baseball great. Then he thought about the older kids he'd spent every afternoon with, the kids who made fun of him if they talked to him at all, the kids who didn't even want him to be there. Josh's vision blurred, and he turned away so his dad wouldn't see his eyes. He wiped them on his sleeve as he left the room, mumbling his good-nights.

The sleep he wanted so badly wouldn't come. The sloped ceiling above the head of his bed never seemed so close, and his tiny room never seemed so small. The dresser and fully stuffed bookshelf that stood shoulder to shoulder alongside his bed seemed to press in on him. Clothes bulged from the narrow closet, forcing its single door open to bump against the bed's footboard. Sports posters hung crowded together on what little wall space he had, and the players seemed to pile out of them into the room and breathe up all the dusty air. Around and around his mind went, half of him hoping he'd make the Titans, the other half hoping he'd be cut and the whole thing could finally be over.

CHAPTER TWENTY

AT LUNCH THE NEXT day, Josh got his milks lined up and looked around for Jaden. If anyone could cheer him up, it was her. Her knowledge of the game and about everything else made her praise of his baseball skills twice as meaningful as anyone else's outside his dad's. He didn't see her, though, and he started in on his first sandwich, not wanting to get behind.

When Benji arrived with a tray of pizza and carrot sticks, Josh asked, "You seen Jaden?"

Benji set down his tray and said, "Who cares?"

"Come on, Lido," Josh said. "She helped you with math, right? You got something like an eighty-one on the quiz? You're out of the woods now. You're going to pass."

Benji puffed out his cheeks and blew air through a

small hole between his lips. "You think that's 'cause of *her*? I got brains just like the rest of you."

"Man, sometimes you really get to me, Lido," Josh said.

"So, you're got," Lido said, picking up his tray and walking away.

"Where you going?" Josh asked.

Benji turned and said, "To sit with some of my *teammates*—the ones who are still left, anyway. Some people around here appreciate me, dude."

Josh watched him go, gulped down the rest of a roast beef sandwich, and searched the lunchroom for Jaden. When he spotted her over by the stage underneath the flag, sitting and eating in the midst of a big group of brainy girls, he balanced his three remaining milks on his lunch bag and crossed the cafeteria.

"Hey," Josh said, nudging Jaden with his hip. "Can you ask someone to make room?"

Jaden looked up at him with a deadpan face.

"No," she said in her southern drawl, "I don't think that's nice."

Josh snorted at the joke and said, "C'mon, Jaden. Stop it. It's me, not Benji. He's mad because I stuck up for you. He's not even sitting with me."

Without looking up at him, Jaden said, "I got to believe that anyone who cares about this school isn't going to be lining up to sit with *you*."

"Hey, easy," Josh said, touching her shoulder. "C'mon,

Jaden. It's not funny anymore."

Jaden shrugged his hand off her shoulder and turned. "I know it's not funny. No one's laughing but you."

"What are you talking about?" Josh asked.

Jaden looked around at her wide-eyed classmates and said, "Fine, you don't care if other people know?"

"Know what? I don't care."

"It was bad enough when your father took you off our baseball team for some pack of muscle-bound all-stars," she said in her drawl, clutching a pretzel so tight it broke into pieces. "I tried to be fair. I tried to be understanding, but I realize now that I did it because of how I feel—how I *felt*—about you. I compromised my journalistic integrity, and I should have known better. Well, fool me once, shame on you. You won't do it twice."

"Twice, how?" Josh asked, his jaw falling.

"Oh, you're going to pretend you don't know?" Jaden said. "Okay, Josh. I believe you. Duh. I'm stupid. You didn't know your dad recruited Kerry Eschelman for the U12 Titans. Sure, I believe you."

Josh stood for a minute, staring at Jaden, then looking around at the other girls' faces and the faces of the kids at the nearby tables staring at him.

"I didn't," he said quietly. "I don't know what you're talking about."

"Right," Jaden said. "I wouldn't want to know either if me and my dad were killing the entire baseball season for the whole school."

"My dad never said anything about Kerry," Josh said, still softly.

"You didn't know he was putting together a U12 travel team?" Jaden asked accusingly. "And he called Kerry's dad, like, twenty times?"

"I . . ." Josh said, not wanting to lie. "I knew about the team, but not Kerry."

"He's only the best seventh-grade pitcher around," Jaden said, slapping the crumbs of her pretzel down on the table in front of her and jumping up so she could stick her face in his. "Only a *moron* wouldn't think they'd go after him. Are you a moron, Josh, or just a liar?"

CHAPTER TWENTY-ONE

JOSH COULDN'T SPEAK. HE clamped his mouth shut, glaring at Jaden, humiliated in front of half the school.

"You're some friend," he said in a mutter. "Benji was right all along. Girls are nothing but trouble."

"Moron it is," Jaden said, the word coming out "MOE-ron," and she turned away and sat back down.

Josh walked away, his ears burning. As he approached the doorway out, his stomach did a backward roll. He dumped the remainder of his lunch, bag and all, into the big trash can.

"Hey," someone behind him said.

Josh turned and frowned when he saw Benji standing there with his tray of garbage.

"Hey," Josh said.

"Your mom give you any of those cookies she

makes?" Benji asked.

"I guess so," Josh said. "Why?"

Benji nodded and dug into the trash can, coming up with Josh's half-empty lunch bag. He fished inside and removed a small Baggie containing three oatmeal-raisin cookies. He took one out and jammed the whole thing into his mouth.

"No sense wasting them," Benji said, chewing as he spoke so it came out half garbled.

Without another word, Benji turned and walked back into the lunchroom. Josh hung his head and made his way toward seventh-period English class.

To make matters worse, his English teacher called on him twice and his social studies teacher three times. He had no idea what to say any of the times. He lost interest in his lessons and could only think about one thing: making the Titans. The half of him that had wanted to return to his friends now knew that he had no friends. The best thing that could happen to Josh would be to make the Mount Olympus Titans and travel the country, honing his skills and letting the world see that no matter what else, he would be a baseball great.

CHAPTER TWENTY-TWO

THE LAST BELL FINALLY rang, and Josh sprinted for the school's main entrance. Outside, clouds surged overhead, and the warm breeze smelled of spring rain. His father waited, as usual, just beyond the buses. After Josh climbed into the car and slammed the door, he slumped down in the seat and stared straight ahead. His father said nothing and put the car into gear, driving off toward the Mount Olympus Sports Complex.

After a time his father said, "Would you really want me to force you onto this team? Have them keep you because I'm your dad?"

Josh kept his lips rolled tight against his teeth.

"Tell me," his father said. "I doubt Rocky will do it, but I can sure try. If it means that much to you, Josh, I'll do it."

Josh let his face relax. He sighed deeply and shook his head.

"No," he said, then let silence have its way again.

"Because—" his dad began to say.

"Dad, did you recruit Kerry Eschelman away from the school team?" Josh said, blurting out the question.

His father glanced at him and nodded his head. "Of course I did. I told you Rocky had me working on putting a team together. I got Silven from Liverpool and Macauly from Solvay, too. Supposedly the three best twelve-year-old pitchers in the city. Why?"

"You ruined the Grant team," Josh said, his eyes on the road straight ahead.

"What about Eschelman?" his father asked. "You think about him? His talent? He could be a college player with the right development."

"Weight lifting and Super Stax?" Josh asked.

"In a couple years, if he's still there. When the time is right," his father said. "I told you—you're different. You're way more advanced."

"Well, we'll see if I am, right?" Josh said, looking over at his father. "And if I'm not, I'm going to play Titans U12."

"And they'd be damn lucky to have you, Josh," his father said.

"'Cause I can't play with the school team anymore."

"You think Coach Miller knows a bat from a bunt?" his dad said.

Josh clamped his mouth shut and looked out the window.

"Looks like rain," Josh said.

"Another good thing about practicing in the bubble," his dad said as they pulled into the circle. "You see that limo?"

Josh looked at the Cadillac stretch limo, so clean it reflected the trees and the cloudy sky above.

"What's that?" Josh asked.

"Sponsors," his father said. "From Nike."

"Nike sneakers?" Josh asked.

"And cleats, and sportswear," his father said. "They're breaking into baseball equipment—gloves, balls, maybe even bats. They're sponsoring five travel teams across the country at every level. Rocky's signing the contract with them today. If I get this U12 thing put together and looking good, he says we might get them to do that deal, too."

"What kind of deal?" Josh asked.

"They pay Rocky a hundred and twenty thousand dollars a year to manage it, plus the team's expenses, coaches, practice facility—the entire budget," his father said. "That means Rocky gets to pay himself for having the team practice at Olympus."

"Wow," Josh said.

"Not a bad business, huh?" his father said. "All right, you get going. And Josh?"

"Yeah, Dad?"

"You're my boy. Be great."

Josh jumped out and scooted inside with the rest of the players. If he didn't make it, it wouldn't be because he didn't try. He growled and yelled his way through his weight workout in a way that made the other kids steal glances at him. When they hit the field, he blew everyone away in the agilities and fired his throws to first so hard, he saw Jones wince at least twice. When he got into the batting cage, he attacked the ball, smashing it wildly around without concern for where it went, only wanting to bust its yellow rubber seams.

Sprints came, and Josh blew their doors in. No one bothered griping at him because no one could catch their breath to do it. Rocky came out of his office as they finished running. When he called them in, Josh gasped for breath himself but kept his head high. He watched as Rocky huddled up outside the half circle of players with his three assistant coaches, whispering among themselves. If Josh didn't make it, he wasn't going to have anything to be ashamed of. Still, his stomach jumped when Rocky cleared his throat.

"As I said a couple weeks ago," Rocky said, "we only keep eighteen. That's all we have room for, and that's the way it is. The other coaches and I got together on this, and we all agree. We also think it's important to make this announcement as a team. For the guy who didn't make it, well, I hope you'll use it as a valuable lesson when you're trying to do it to it in other areas of life. I know you'll have other opportunities to do things down the road, and it's important that you use this experience as a lesson to motivate you to work even harder."

Rocky looked Josh directly in the eye, and Josh stopped breathing.

"The guy who didn't make it is . . ." Rocky said, and cleared his throat.

Josh closed his eyes.

CHAPTER TWENTY-THREE

"BOBBY PERKINS," ROCKY SAID. "Sorry, Perkins. You tried your best."

Perkins inhaled so quick it became a sob. He hid his face in the crook of his arm, stood up, and walked off the field, his shoulders shuddering so hard that Josh felt bad for the kid. A sudden burst of elation buried his pity, and Josh had to fight to keep his mouth from pulling into a monster smile. He bit down on the inside of his lower lip to keep his composure, but nothing could prevent his eyes from stretching wide with joy.

The sour looks he got from his new teammates dampened his spirits, but they could do nothing more than what a brief rain shower does to an active volcano. Josh searched for his father up in the small set of concrete stands overlooking the field. In the gloomy light underneath the bubble's soiled canvas, his father sat alone with his back straight and his arms crossed in front of his massive frame, like a man defying a snowstorm.

Josh glanced around, then snuck a thumbs-up to his dad.

His dad broke out in a gleaming grin and returned the thumbs-up.

"I don't care if you don't like it," Rocky was saying to the team. "You've got a new teammate. If you don't want to be replaced yourself, you'll treat Josh like he belongs. I don't care about his age. That's not a factor now. He's one of us, and he earned it."

Rocky's three assistants began to applaud, and the kids around Josh joined in unenthusiastically. Rocky seemed not to notice. He winked at Josh and called the team together for their chant of "Do it to it." Josh secretly thought the saying was stupid, but this time he said it with gusto, then jogged off the field to hug his father.

When the two of them separated, Josh's dad said he thought they should celebrate with hot dogs from Heid's. Josh said he'd hurry and made his way into the locker room. Perkins sat in front of his emptied locker with his face buried in his hands. A couple guys tried to talk to Perkins, but he shrugged them away. No one would even look at Josh.

Out in the car, Josh asked his dad, "Did you know all along?"

His father shook his head and said, "I didn't even want to ask. But while you were in the locker room, I talked to Rocky. He said you had it made after the first week, but the way you worked today made the decision even easier."

"What'll happen to Perkins?" Josh asked.

His father shrugged. "That's life, buddy. He can try to find another team or go back and play high school ball next year. Everybody you play with is going to drop out of this sooner or later. The key is for you to stay in, and from what I've seen, that's gonna happen."

"Thanks," Josh said, warm all over even though the rain outside had brought with it a spring chill that seeped into the car.

When they arrived at the hot-dog place, Josh and his dad ordered up four each, dousing them with mustard and relish and mixing big paper cups full of white and chocolate milk together. They sat down in a booth by the window and dug in, talking between bites about the tournament on Long Island and the players his dad had recruited for the two new Titans teams.

After a pause, Josh wiped a glob of mustard from his cheek and asked, "What do you think I should do about the rest of the guys?"

"Meaning what?" his dad asked.

"I mean, Rocky told everyone that I'm part of the team and they should treat me the same as everyone else," Josh said, "but I don't know."

"Don't know if they'll accept you anyway?" his dad asked.

"Yeah."

His dad finished the last bite of his last dog and drank his milk through a straw until slurping sounds filled the air and he set down the cup. He wiped his mouth on a yellow paper napkin and said, "You just ignore it. Pretend like everything's fine."

"Even if it isn't?"

"A team's a funny thing," his dad said. "You can't force your way in; you have to let it happen. The biggest thing you can do is play well. You just keep your mouth shut and do it to it at the tournament this weekend. You'll see. Everything will change. Everybody loves a winner, Josh. Everybody."

CHAPTER TWENTY-FOUR

THE TITANS GOT ON a bus at 2:30 the next day after school. The ride to Long Island took about seven hours, but that included a stop for dinner on the way. Josh sat in a window seat in the back reading, and occasionally gazing out at the rolling green Catskill Mountains. After they crossed the George Washington Bridge, Rocky got on the intercom and announced that in a couple minutes they'd be passing the new Yankee Stadium on the left. The bus fell quiet.

Josh cupped his hands and put his face to the window. The sun had dipped behind the clouds, but the stadium glowed with white light, as though a giant treasure lay sparkling within its walls. In fact, it was a treasure, the only true treasure for Josh and his teammates. The heart of Major League Baseball. One of only a handful of places anyone who ever loved the game dreamed they would someday play in.

The bus stayed quiet until they crossed the Triborough Bridge and the towering glitter of Manhattan loomed alongside the dark East River. Chatter about the Empire State Building, the Chrysler Building, and the jets gliding their way through the night as they piled into La Guardia gave the rest of the ride a festive air. The prospect of the morning's competition made them giddy, and as they stepped off the bus and walked into the hotel, laughter rang across the Marriott's lobby.

Rocky handed out the keys, and teammates raced up the side stairs or pestered the elevator button to be first to their rooms for the bed by the window. Josh got his key last and took his time, not caring which bed he slept in because he didn't really expect to sleep. By the time he got to the bank of elevators, he was able to ride his own car up to the second floor. The door to the room stood ajar. Josh peered in, then stepped slowly, wondering who his roommate for the next two nights would be.

The answer couldn't have been worse.

CHAPTER TWENTY-FIVE

"I'M TAKING THE WINDOW." Jones was already laid out on the bed with his shoes still on, staring at the ceiling. He scrunched his pale eyebrows, and the freckles on his cheeks and nose danced in a red soup of anger. In one hand he spun a baseball around and around with the flick of his fingers and wrist.

Josh put his bag on the other bed. He took out a paperback copy of *The Count of Monte Cristo*, fluffed up the pillows, and sat down to read. After a couple minutes, Jones jumped up and walked out, spinning the ball in one hand.

"And don't touch my stuff," Jones said on his way, slamming the door.

Josh stared at the closed door for a moment, sighed, and returned to his book. At ten, a knock on the door preceded Moose, who stuck his head into the room and asked where Jones was. Josh shrugged. Moose looked at him blankly for a moment, then disappeared. Several minutes later the door flew open and Jones stormed into the room, throwing himself down on the bed. Moose shook his head and told them to turn out the lights before saying good-night.

Josh looked at his older teammate, waiting to see what he'd do. Jones yanked two pillows free from under the bedspread, sandwiched his head between them, and turned to face the window.

"You heard him," Jones said, still facing the window. "Turn the lights off."

Josh sighed again and went to use the bathroom and brush his teeth. By the time he got out, Jones had begun to snore.

Josh kept the light on and lost himself in his book, finally falling asleep sometime after Edmond Dantès escaped from prison and had a knife fight with pirates on the Isle of Monte Cristo. He woke to the sound of Jones banging around in the bathroom. The book lay open on his chest. Jones emerged from the bathroom in full uniform. He pulled his cap on tight, picked up his glove, and walked out of the room without a word.

Josh got ready, too, and made his way downstairs to the dining room, where most of the team had already sat down to a breakfast buffet. Josh put a scoop of scrambled eggs on a plate along with some cantaloupe and a Danish. He filled a glass with juice, then took a seat in a booth by himself. From the corner of his eye, he watched his teammates, all of them apparently as nervous as he was. Rocky sat as silent as a block of marble in a corner booth surrounded by his coaches.

When the coaches rose from their table, the rest of the team followed without speaking, and they streamed out through the lobby and onto the waiting bus. As they rode toward the Garden City Town Park, the sun poked its nose above the rooftops, blinding Josh with its early rays. He looked away, blinking. They turned a corner, and there lay the green fields, spread far and wide across more than a dozen acres of flatland amid the buildings and houses of the small city.

Two other buses were already in the parking lot, and the Titans' bus pulled up alongside them. Waiting in the back of the bus while the others unloaded, Josh spotted a silver Taurus pull into the parking lot, pass their bus, and come to rest in a spot near the concession stand. The warmth of familiarity filled his chest before his father emerged from the old Taurus. Even three hundred miles from home he'd sensed—rather than actually seen—the dent in the rear bumper and the white scrape of paint where his mother had nicked the garage. Still, his smile didn't break loose until he saw his father's face under the shadow of his thick black hair and eyebrows, darkened even more by stubble from a nightlong drive.

By the time Josh stepped out onto the pavement, his father stood close enough to shake his hand, which he did.

"How'd you get here?" Josh asked, knowing Rocky had assigned him to a business dinner with the athletic director of a Syracuse-area college the night before.

His father rubbed at the stubble on his chin and grinned in an apologetic way—a way Josh wasn't used to—and said, "I wasn't going to miss your debut when the only thing between us was a couple extra-large coffees."

Josh hugged his father, burying his nose in the comforting smell of his denim shirt.

Josh jumped at the sound of Rocky's whistle and hustled off toward the field, where the team had already begun to warm up. Josh nearly forgot about his father when their first opponent, the Hempstead Eagles, arrived. He gawked at the sight of their players. They had a pitcher taller than Jones and a catcher with muscles as big as Tucker's. While Josh had grown used to the size and muscles of his teammates, it seemed almost frightening to see the same thing in kids he didn't know.

The other thing Josh couldn't stop marveling at was the distance of the outfield fence. Because the Titans practiced inside, Josh hadn't yet played on a regulation field. He'd been an occasional batboy for the Syracuse Chiefs and always thought the distance of the outfield fence was something only a grown man such as his father wouldn't find intimidating. All the home runs Josh had hit in his life up till now had been in parks where the fence stood about two hundred feet from home plate. The field on which they were getting ready to play looked twice as big.

When it came his turn to warm up his bat on some ball tosses hit into the backstop, Josh asked Moose how far it was to the fence.

Moose tugged on the bill of his cap, looked down the first-base line, and said, "Looks like three twenty. Why?"

"No reason," Josh said, swallowing and turning his attention to the drill.

When Rocky called the team together, his voice rasped as if he'd been up shouting all night.

"I didn't tell you this until now, but our scouting report says this team we're about to play is going to be the best competition we'll face," Rocky said. "We got a bad draw, but if we can beat these guys, this tournament will be ours. Trust me, it's a big step in getting to our goal of the Junior Olympics. So, all we do today is do it to it. That's what we do, we do it to it and we're on our way."

Rocky's small, dark eyes glittered like black beetle wings.

"So, I want every single one of you to dig deep," Rocky said, gritting his teeth and letting his eyes come to rest on Josh. "We worked too hard to lose this thing, and we're too good. But we can't be soft. We can't make excuses about why we didn't play our best. You *have* to play your best. You have to *be* the best. If you can't go out there in a game like this and perform, then you'll never be great. And if you can't be great, then you're wasting your time, and mine. Let's go."

CHAPTER TWENTY-SIX

BEFORE HE KNEW IT, Josh found himself on the baseline with his hat over his heart listening to "The Star Spangled Banner" scratched out by a small cluster of speakers on a pole behind the backstop. The flag hung limp in the center of all four baseball fields, and after the anthem, an announcer welcomed everyone to the twenty-third Garden City U14 Baseball Tournament.

Both teams put their hats back on. The Titans took the field first. Josh stood rigid at shortstop and threw off target during warm-ups, but no one—except his father, who stood in the back row of the bleachers clutching a Titans cap—seemed to notice him. Thankfully, Kyle Watson, their starting pitcher, put down the first three batters and Josh jogged with everyone else, cheering, into the dugout.

Josh saw the lineup chart hanging on the fence. He batted sixth, one in front of Jones. While the Titans' first man up struck out, the next two got on base. Then Tucker, their cleanup batter, struck out—swinging big to try to bring in some runs but struggling against the pitcher's wicked curveball. Josh tugged on his left-hand batting glove, found a helmet and his favorite bat, and walked to the on-deck circle. Watson stepped up to the plate. Mostly, Josh wanted Watson to get a hit so they could score and win, but a small, cowardly part of him knew that if Watson struck out, then Josh wouldn't have to bat.

Josh swung his bat idly, trying to let his body absorb its weight, but he was distracted by the odd throwing motion of the Eagles' left-handed pitcher and the sight of his father, who had moved from the bleachers to the backstop and hung on the chain-link fence with his fingers hooked through the steel mesh. With a 3–2 count, Watson swung at a curveball and hit it foul. Josh's hand felt hot inside the glove, and his sweat made it sticky. On the next pitch, Watson swung at another curveball and dribbled it just outside the third-base line. He was still alive.

Two more times Watson protected the plate before he let a high fastball go and the umpire called ball four. Watson dumped his bat at Josh's feet on his way to first. The other batters advanced, loading up the bases with two outs.

Rocky stepped out of the dugout and put a hand

on Josh's shoulder. One of the veins in Rocky's neck throbbed, and Josh nearly choked on the heavy smell of the coach's cologne mixed with the chewing tobacco on his breath.

"You gonna bat lefty?" Rocky asked.

Josh looked at the glove on his left hand and said, "You want me to, right?"

"You don't need to knock it out," Rocky said, tightening his grip and drawing Josh's eyes into his own. "Just get me a hit and an RBI. One run at a time. With their bats and the way we play defense, we could beat this team one–nothing, so don't swing big. Just get me a run."

Josh nodded, and Rocky let go. As he approached the batter's box, Josh heard his father's urgent words coming to him through the backstop.

"Swing big on the fastball, Josh," his father said. "That'll be his first pitch. He's not gonna like seeing you on the left side of the plate. His magic curveball is nothing against a lefty. You can do it!"

Josh's legs seemed numb, and his arms felt heavier than they should have. He nodded at his father, acknowledging that he'd heard the words of advice, even though they contradicted his coach's. The eggs and half of the Danish he'd eaten rolled around on the inside of his gut. Part of it made a dash for his throat, but he gulped it down and stepped up to the plate with a wary eye on the pitcher.

The pitcher smiled at him and went into his jerky

motion. Josh saw the ball and knew it was all heat, right down the pipe. He knew he should swing big—like his father said—and drive it out of the park, but Rocky's words jumped into his mind. He swung down on the ball, but late, and missed. The Eagles infield erupted with cheers. Silence sat heavy in the Titans dugout. The second pitch, a changeup, dropped real low—a ball—which was a good thing since Josh stood frozen in place, too flustered to concentrate.

"Swing big!" his father yelled.

"Loosen up!" Moose shouted at him.

Another changeup came at him. He saw it leave the pitcher's hand with a forward spin. He swung down on it, trying for the hole between first and second, knowing that his father would want him to follow his coach's direction before all else. He connected, but too soon, and the ball went foul way outside the third-base line.

Josh stepped out of the box. With a 1–2 count, he knew what would come before he even heard his father's voice.

"Fastball. Fastball," his father said.

Josh could see the smirk on the pitcher's horse-shaped face, and he knew his father was right. More than anything, he wanted to swing big. He looked out at the fence. It seemed a mile away. But with all his lifting and training, why couldn't he reach it? His instincts told him to do it, and he remembered something his father had said to him about instincts and—

"Let's go," the umpire said to Josh.

Josh nodded and stepped up to the plate. He glanced at the loaded bases, then at the two outs up on the scoreboard. The pitcher reared back and jerked sideways. His arm whipped around and came Josh's way. Most people would see it like they'd see a snake flick its tongue, but Josh saw more. The ball left the pitcher's hand with a perfect spin, a fastball to the outside edge of the plate.

Josh swung big, and connected with a crack.

The ball took off.

CHAPTER TWENTY-SEVEN

THE TITANS DUGOUT ERUPTED, and Josh's heart swelled on his way down the first-base line. He kept his eye on the ball, which was screaming with the perfect arc for the right-field fence. Instead of watching the ball go over his head, the right fielder sprinted all-out for the fence. Josh felt a pang of doubt as the ball began to fall.

It *had* to make it. He'd hit it as hard as he'd ever hit anything.

Still, the outfielder ran right at the fence as if it were made of pillows instead of chain-link steel. The ball kept dropping. Josh rounded first. The outfielder turned—five feet short of the fence—and snapped the ball from the air.

"Crap!" Rocky shouted somewhere behind Josh.

Josh motored down and turned toward the dugout

with his head hung. As he passed Rocky, the coach's words seethed from his mouth.

"I said get me a *hit*," Rocky said. "You think this is Little League and you're some big star? You're *one* player on this team, big shot. Now get out there."

Josh choked back his tears, and Rocky turned his back. Josh unloaded his batting helmet and picked up his mitt, going through the motions as if in a bad dream. Numb, he trotted out to his position at shortstop and tried hard to focus on warming up as Moose peppered balls around the infield. He watched with a knotted stomach as Rocky walked casually to the backstop and the place where his father gripped the fence. The two of them spoke, with Rocky gesturing his hands and Josh's father nodding slightly, until his father turned and made his way back to the bleachers, where he stood with his mouth clamped shut.

Through the innings to come, Josh recovered his wits and played well on defense, twice scooping up hot grounders and throwing runners out at first. Once he even backpedaled a good twenty feet to snag a pop fly. Through the noise, he could hear his father's cries of joy, and it swelled Josh's heart, reviving him completely. He kept his swing down the next time he got up and hit a line-drive single over second base but never scored. The third time up, he grounded out to second. In the fifth, the Eagles changed to a pitcher who threw more heat than their starter and put down the first three batters—two of them at the top of the Titans' lineup—as if they were Little League washouts. At the bottom of the sixth and final inning, there was still no score. The Titans' first batter struck out.

Tucker got up and on a 2–2 count drove a fastball into the fence. The center fielder pulled it out of the bounce and made a sensational cutoff to the shortstop. Tucker held at second. Rocky conferred with Moose, then traded signals with the third-base coach, who in turn signaled Tucker. Tucker jammed his helmet down tight on his head and set his jaw. The Titans' big catcher crouched, ready to run, the cords in his neck taut and his fists balled.

Rocky whispered something to Watson, who strode to the plate. Josh pulled on his batting glove and helmet and waited in the on-deck circle, slowly swinging his bat and studying the motion of the new pitcher. The pitcher wound up, and Watson went into a bunting stance. The pitcher threw a curveball that Watson dribbled down the first-base line. Tucker took off from second.

The catcher threw his mask in the air. Before the mask hit the dirt, he pounced on the ball and gunned it to the outstretched first baseman. Watson never had a chance, but Tucker now stood bouncing on third, clapping his hands and growling like a red-faced maniac. The dugout went wild. Josh took a deep breath.

Rocky gripped both of Josh's shoulders and brought

his face so close, their noses almost touched.

"Just a hit," Rocky said, his dark, close-set eyes glinting under the eaves of a scowl. "No heroics. Swing down on it and hit a hole. You gotta get us a hit. Do it to it, Josh. Be great."

Josh breathed deep again and nodded. Rocky sent him off toward the plate, and Josh told himself over and over to swing down on the ball no matter what kind of pitch came at him. Up in the stands, Josh's father gave him a tight nod. When Josh stepped up to the batter's box on the left-hand side of the plate, he looked down the third-base line. Instead of sneering, Tucker pressed his lips together, nodding silently and giving Josh a thumbs-up. The muscles in Tucker's giant forearm rippled. Josh bit his lower lip and looked out at the pitcher on the mound.

The pitcher nodded and wound up. The first pitch—a fastball—nicked the outside of the plate. Josh let it go, and the umpire called it a strike. Rocky groaned and chattered at the umpire. Josh dug in.

The second pitch came. All heat and a bit high, a pitch Josh could put out of the park. He raised up and tried to swing down on it, nicking the ball and sending it foul, up and over the backstop behind him. Josh stepped out of the box and took a deep breath, trying to push the 0–2 count into the back of his mind and think only about the next pitch.

"You can do it, Josh!" Tucker screamed from third

base, the cords in his thick neck bulging along with the muscles that ran from his shoulders up behind his ears. The Hempstead Eagles fans were on their feet in the small metal stands, stamping and cheering. His own team stood, ready to gush from the dugout or melt into a blob of depression.

The pitcher reared back and raised his left foot as if to stomp the mound. His hand came out of his glove from behind his back, lashing past his ear and releasing the pitch.

The ball came out of his hand dead center and hot, the perfect pitch to swing big on, to knock out of the park.

Josh cranked back his coiled arms and hips ever so slightly, just a bit more torque for a bit more power.

The ball zipped at him like the blink of a bullet.

He swung.

CHAPTER TWENTY-EIGHT

THE BAT CRACKED. THE pitcher jumped as if he'd stepped on a nail, and the ball hit the mound at his feet before shooting almost straight up. Josh took off for first, digging his cleats into the dirt. From the corner of his eye he was aware of Tucker, streaking like a big blur, nearly halfway home.

The ball seemed to float a hundred feet above the mound, then dropped like a rock. Josh kept churning, knowing it would be an easy throw to first when the ball returned to earth and that the shortstop had moved into position to make the play.

Josh ran. The ball hit the shortstop's glove, and the throw came. Josh's foot hit the bag, and the first baseman snapped up the throw from the shortstop with a pop. Josh ran through the bag and twisted around. The umpire crouched, still staring at the bag, processing what he saw and what he heard. Josh held his breath.

"Safe!"

The dugout exploded, and the Titans swarmed Josh. Tucker beat them all and hugged Josh and lifted him up over his head, dancing around and screaming madly. The rest of the players reached up, their fingers stretched toward him. Josh touched their hands, slapping fives and grasping fingers, Tucker whirling him around all the while.

CHAPTER TWENTY-NINE

THE ALARM WENT OFF. Josh rolled out of bed and let the radio play while he dressed. They hadn't returned from Long Island until after midnight, and Josh had to rub his eyes and search his memory to make sure the whole weekend hadn't been some strange dream. Then he saw it.

Standing tall on his dresser, the golden figure of a baseball player, his bat at the ready and nearly tickling the slanted ceiling, was perched atop a marble platform. That platform rested on four gold columns, stretching more than a foot to an even bigger marble base below. The nameplate read GARDEN CITY CHAMPIONS, and the whole trophy glowed like a beacon in the dim gray light of the tiny bedroom.

Josh cradled the trophy in his arms and ran his

fingers up and down the smooth grooves in the long columns. He let the golden figure lie along the side of his cheek as he remembered the hits and the grabs and the throws and the cheers and the smiles and the claps on his back. He remembered the long ride home singing "One Hundred Bottles of Beer on the Wall" and the sight of his father's silver Taurus darting in and out of traffic, sometimes alongside the bus, sometimes ahead or behind, but always there, the way a pilot fish will stay with a shark.

Josh used the bathroom, flushing the toilet—which sent a shiver through the pipes, rattling them down into the walls of the kitchen below. He brushed his teeth, smelling his parents' coffee and hearing the low murmur of their voices floating up the narrow stairs. After changing into jeans and the bright green T-shirt that came with the trophy, Josh skipped down the stairs and stopped just outside the kitchen at the sudden yells coming from within.

"And *I* say you should have let the boy get his rest," his father said. "That's more important than school. I turned off his alarm for a reason."

"Really?" his mother said, her voice grating like nails on a chalkboard.

"He can be *great*, Laura," his father said.

"*You* were great," his mother said. "He needs school. He needs to go to college."

"You're going to bring *me* into this?" his father shouted,

banging the kitchen table so that the silverware and the sugar bowl rattled. "Thanks, Laura. Thanks for the reminder that I didn't make it. Thanks for the reminder that I'm a vitamin salesman. Have a nice day."

Josh heard the scrape of a chair, heavy steps, and then the kitchen door swinging open before it slammed shut, causing Josh's little sister to wail like a car alarm. Josh covered his ears and walked through the doorway to see his mother scoop Laurel out of her high chair. His mother held her close and stroked the back of her head.

"Hurry up, Josh," his mother said. "You'll miss the bus. Look at the paper, though."

"Okay," Josh said, taking a box of Cheerios from the cupboard and pouring some milk into a bowl.

He sat down at the place where his father had been and the sports section lay.

"Hey, wow," Josh said, stopping to swallow. "That's me."

On the front page was a color picture of Josh in an openmouthed scream, being carried by his teammates after the big win over Hempstead. The headline read VALENTINE'S TITANS JUST THAT. The caption talked about Josh being only twelve and knocking in the winning run to upset the fifth-ranked U14 team in the country.

"Your father took the picture and sent it in," his mother said, jiggling Josh's sister to calm her as she paced the kitchen floor.

"You sound mad about it," Josh said, shoveling in another mouthful of cereal.

"I'm not mad," his mother said, replacing his sister in her high chair and peeling a banana to give her. "I just want to make sure you've got your priorities straight. All this baseball is fine, but you need to do well in school. That's what matters. Your father turned your alarm off, but I put it back on so you wouldn't be late."

Josh shrugged, gulped down a glass of juice, and said, "Okay."

"Because that's what matters," she said as if he'd contradicted her. "Look at your father. He was a first-round draft pick. Now he's working for Rocky Valentine."

"What's wrong with Coach Valentine?" Josh asked.

His mother cleared some dirty dishes off the table and began banging them around in the sink.

"I didn't say anythinig was," his mother said, clattering a spoon into a bowl. "He's fine. I'm sure he's a good coach. Obviously. But he's an operator and not the kind of person you want to have to work for."

"What do you mean, 'an operator'?" Josh asked.

"Are you done yet?" his mother asked, glancing up at the clock. "It's time."

Josh jumped up from the table, put his things together, kissed his little sister and his mom, and dashed out the door. When he stepped onto the bus he saw Jaden sitting in the second seat. Josh always sat in the front row for several reasons. First, no one wanted the front seat, so he never had to argue about it. Second, he sometimes got carsick in the back. Third, the opportunity for trouble of any kind was reduced to zero if the person right beside you was Mrs. Wamp, the bus driver. He didn't relish sitting right in front of Jaden, but he wasn't going to give up the comfort of the front.

Avoiding her eyes, he took his seat. The bus doors hissed and banged shut. The gears ground and off they went. Before the next stop, Josh felt a tap on his shoulder. He looked back. Jaden didn't look at him, but she dumped the folded sports section of the morning paper over the back of his seat and into his lap.

"Congratulations," she said, speaking the words as though someone were jamming a spoonful of nasty medicine into her mouth at the same time.

Josh sat looking forward. His fingers closed around the paper and he tapped it lightly against his other hand, thinking. Finally, without turning, he said, "Thanks."

Josh couldn't help smiling to himself the whole ride to school. Every other person who got on flashed their eyes his way, offering up a knowing nod that told him they, too, had seen the big sports page and his picture. When the bus finally pulled up in front of Grant Middle, Josh almost waited for Jaden to catch up to him. Something about Jaden tugged at him the way a campfire drew him close on a dark night in the woods, and he felt as if the newspaper was a peace offering and that she'd talk to him again.

But when Josh turned, Jaden didn't get off the bus after he did. He saw her sitting there with her arms crossed as if she was mad that he hadn't shown more appreciation for her congratulations. So Josh shrugged and headed for his locker, where Benji stood, bouncing on his toes.

"Hey, dude," Benji said.

Josh just looked at him, then spun the dial on his lock.

"Congrats, my man," Benji said, patting Josh on the back. "Front page of the sports section. I had breakfast at Denny's with my dad this morning. He said you're on your way. His exact words. What do you think about that, huh?"

Benji's dad worked on the line at a plastics factory, but he also played for the Salt City Express, Syracuse's semi-pro football team. Even though Benji's dad lived on the other side of town and didn't spend that much time with him, Benji still considered his dad the ulti-mate authority on sports. Josh had gone to a couple of Express games with Benji. Along with a crowd of about fifty other people, he'd seen Mr. Lido manhandle the opposing teams' defensive linemen. Even Josh's father talked about how Mr. Lido had been a starter at Ohio State before he blew out his knee, so the praise carried some real weight for Josh, and he couldn't keep from beaming at his friend.

"He said so, even if I'm not your teammate?" Josh said, teasing him.

"Aw," Benji said, brushing away the words with a flick of his wrist, "you and me don't hold grudges. I'm no hater, and neither are you. Speaking of teammates, I want you to talk to your dad about getting me on that U12 team with Esch. They could use my skills, and my dad says that's the path to the big leagues. You can have all the talent in the world, but you gotta have the right training. I figured he meant me when he said it."

Josh took his books from the locker and glanced over at his friend.

"Right," Josh said.

Josh still felt anger at Benji, but his friend's silly smile and enthusiasm were quickly melting it away.

"Oh, dude, there's the bell," Benji said. "See you in math."

Ms. Huxter didn't give them time for anything in math except common denominators, so Benji didn't get to really pester Josh about the U12 team until lunch. He started in right away, and even though Josh told him he'd do his best, Benji didn't let it go. He kept listing his unique skills for Josh and demanding that he repeat them so that when Sheila Conway set her tray down on the other side of him, Josh forgot to be terrified.

CHAPTER THIRTY

"HI, JOSH," SHEILA SAID, splitting open a carton of milk and removing a pear from her bag. With her golden hair pulled tight into a ponytail, she looked even prettier than usual.

Benji blinked at Josh from across the table, his mouth open, and miraculously silent.

"Hi," Josh said, coughing up the word from the bottom of his lungs.

Sheila turned the pear, studying it before taking a small bite and saying, "I heard you broke up with Jaden."

Josh looked at Benji, whose mouth now opened and closed like a goldfish's.

"I, uh," Josh said, stuttering, "n-never was going out with her to begin with."

Sheila looked at him with pale blue eyes as cool and motionless as the ones in the glass cat his mother kept on a little shelf beside the kitchen clock. They reflected the light like jewels, or tiny shards of broken mirror.

"I'm so glad," she said.

Josh swallowed even though his bologna and lettuce sandwich remained suspended halfway to his mouth without a fresh bite since she'd sat down. He glanced across the lunchroom and saw Jaden sitting by herself in the far corner.

"Because I broke up with Bart," Sheila said. "I did it yesterday. I mean, it didn't have anything to do with your picture in the paper. I want you to know that. He's too controlling."

Josh heard some air escape Benji. He looked down at his sandwich, willing it toward his mouth. He had no idea what she meant, but it wouldn't do to say so. If he could only take a bite, he'd have something to do other than gawk at those eyes.

"So, I was thinking," Sheila said without so much as a glance at Benji, "you and I could go out now."

Benji squeaked and stuck a knuckle into his mouth, nodding at Josh to say yes, but Josh couldn't say anything. He couldn't eat. He couldn't talk. It took every ounce of will he had just to keep breathing. He was both thrilled by the direct attention of the beautiful older girl and horrified by the thought of what her ex-boyfriend might do.

Sheila munched at her pear, taking small sips from her milk between bites. Benji began to eat again, chewing wildly, his eyes darting from Josh to Sheila and back again as though he were watching a tennis match. When she finally finished, Sheila stuffed her empty milk carton and the core of her pear into her lunch bag before reaching out and covering the back of Josh's left hand.

He went rigid, but she only patted his hand and said, "This is going to be so cool. You're so cute, Josh. I love how you're just quiet and cute."

Josh watched her get up and walk away. Benji pounded the table with his fist.

"Dude, you are so going out with her!" Benji said. "She is the bomb! Sheila Conway! Dude, you are my hero!"

CHAPTER THIRTY-ONE

JOSH FELT THE BLOOD return to his face, red hot, and he glanced around, horrified at the staring faces.

"Be quiet," he told Benji.

"No, dude, it is so cool. She asked *you* out. She's the bomb!"

"Be quiet, Benji," Josh hissed, grabbing his friend's wrist as he glanced all around. "I'm *not* going out with her."

"You so are," Benji said, laughing. "And she is so hot. Ow, dude! That hurts."

"Stop it!" Josh said, tightening his grip.

"Jeez," Benji said, pulling away. "You act like you caught a disease. Are you nuts?"

"I am *not* going out with her," Josh said, keeping his voice low. "I am not going out with anyone. Why? Why

135

would I do that? What does that mean?"

"I don't know," Benji said, rubbing his wrist and looking hurt. "You hold her hand. You go to the dance with her. You send her a couple notes and text message her on a daily basis. Maybe you kiss her, dude."

Josh felt a chill go through him, and he shook his head. "I didn't say anything."

"But she did," Benji said. "And you didn't say no, and who would believe it if you did?"

"She's got a boyfriend who was ready to kill me when I *wasn't* going out with her," Josh said.

"You'll crush that guy," Benji said. "He's a beanpole. You'll snap his neck like a candy cane."

"Would you stop that, Benji?" Josh said. "Just stop it. Do you think this is a movie? Do you think I'm Bruce Willis or something? This is *real*. That guy's gonna come after me."

"The only way to stop a bully is to punch him right in the mouth," Benji said. "That's what my dad says. That's why you don't see anyone giving him any cheap shots on the football field. *Bam*. Right in the mouth. That's what my dad does."

"I'm not your dad," Josh said.

The bell rang, and Josh threw his half-eaten sandwich down on the cellophane wrapper.

"I didn't even get to eat," he said.

Benji grinned at him, held up both hands palms up, shrugged, and said, "You don't need food, man. You can be like Romeo and live on love."

"*Bam*," Josh said, extending his fist into the air between them.

"What's that?" Benji asked.

"For you," Josh said, letting his fist drop. "Right in your mouth."

"Save it for Bart," Benji said, still smiling and giving Josh's arm a friendly squeeze. "You'll need it."

CHAPTER THIRTY-TWO

IF THE TITANS THOUGHT Rocky would ease up on their practices after the big win, they were wrong. Monday and Tuesday left Josh so sore and tired that his mom had to dump a Dixie cup of cold water on his head to get him up on Wednesday morning, and he had to take three aspirins before he could pick up his cereal spoon. In math class, he actually fell asleep until Ms. Huxter's ruler exploded off his desktop.

"Dude," Benji said, tagging along as they moved through the hallway toward lunch, "what's up?"

Josh groaned and told him that Rocky was trying to kill them.

"Don't you have another tournament this weekend?" Benji asked. "Did you know the U12 team has its tryouts Saturday?"

Josh glanced at him. "Yes, we have a tournament, and why wouldn't I know about the tryouts? I'm the one who begged my dad just to get you into those tryouts."

"Aw," Benji said, waving his hand, "he was gonna ask me anyway, you know that. A hitter like me?"

Josh shook his head.

"Anyway," Benji said, "my point is, Rocky will probably start taking it easy on you guys now with the tourney coming up on Saturday."

"I hope so," Josh said.

As she did on Monday and Tuesday, Sheila plunked herself down right next to Josh at lunch and started talking to him as if she'd known him for years. He'd grown used to her presence enough to eat and even had worked up the courage to respond to her questions with a muted yes or no. The one question he wanted to ask he could never seem to get out: How was Bart handling the breakup?

Josh still insisted to anyone who asked that he wasn't going out with her, but no one listened. Jaden wouldn't even look at him, and on the bus ride to school, he saw her in the back, one time trading shoves with one of the regular troublemakers before cracking open her book.

On the way to practice, Josh's dad talked excitedly about a sale he'd made to supply the baseball team at the local community college with a year's supply of Super Stax.

"Do you know that if this Nike deal goes through, I

could make more money working for Rocky in one year than I averaged in my last four seasons?" his dad said. "They're talking now about sponsoring the U12 team, too."

"Great."

"But nothing like what you'll make in the big leagues, buddy," his father said excitedly. "I just want to be your agent."

"Sure, Dad."

His dad reached over and tousled his hair. When they arrived at Mount Olympus Sports, Josh hopped out and dashed inside, only to find the locker room empty except for Moose, looking grim.

"Just head out to the field," Moose said.

"But lifting," Josh said.

Moose angled his head toward the door that led to the field and said, "You don't need your stuff."

Josh's insides tightened, and he walked through the locker room in a trance, trying to figure out what he'd done wrong, frantically searching the past few days for something that could have resulted in his being let go. It didn't seem possible.

When he swung open the door, he breathed a sigh of relief at the sight of the rest of the team, also in their school clothes, in a half circle around Rocky. Josh took a knee and waited. Two more players came out after him, and Rocky cleared his throat.

"Do it to it," Rocky said. "That's what you did in Garden City."

Instead of smiling, Rocky scowled as he continued. "But instead of letting you pat yourselves on the back, I wanted to see how you'd respond to some tough sessions. Well, you did good. You did real good, and so today, we're gonna have some fun."

Rocky's assistants broke out in smiles, and even Rocky himself looked kind of happy.

"Instead of working your tails off again, I rented out the laser tag place at Destiny USA."

Josh joined the rest of the team, hooting and clapping his hands.

"We got a couple vans, so load 'em up and move 'em out," Rocky said, pointing a finger in the air and lowering it like a loaded pistol toward the front doors before firing with his thumb. "Do it to it."

Josh followed the surge of players out the doorway and piled into the second van with eight other guys, Moose, and another assistant. When they got to the mall, Josh suited up in his laser pack and dove into the maze with a whoop. The team chose up sides and played hard, running for cover, sprinting in all-out assaults, and dodging enemy fire. By the time it was over and Rocky led them toward the food court, sweat drenched Josh's shirt. He spotted the restrooms off to one side. He told Moose where he was going, and the coach asked Josh if he wanted fries and a soda. Josh said Sprite would be great and that he'd be right back.

Josh walked into the bathroom and smelled the stink of cigarette smoke right away, then saw a little cloud float up from one of the stalls. He wrinkled his nose but stepped up to a urinal, eager to get back. When the door to the smoky stall banged open, Josh looked up into the mirror from washing his hands.

"Well, well, well, I come to the mall looking for a new hoody and what do I find? A little rat who likes sniffing where he shouldn't, a rat gonna get snapped up in a trap. Smack, like that."

Josh spun around, then backed up, bumping the sink—no place to go.

Bart Wilson had him cornered.

CHAPTER THIRTY-THREE

WITHOUT ANOTHER WORD, BART grabbed a handful of Josh's sweaty T-shirt and flung him backward into the stall. The door crashed in and Josh stumbled, slipping on the slick floor, lucky to catch himself on the toilet, his head missing the pipe by an inch.

"Fight me, don't fight me," Bart said, growling and grabbing for Josh. "I don't care. I'm wiping the floor with you, you little rat."

Josh gritted his teeth and shook his head. Instead of turning away, he steadied himself, clenched his hand into a fist, and reared it back like he was going to throw to first base.

When a hand appeared from nowhere and snatched Bart by the collar out of the doorway to the stall, Josh froze in amazement, still balanced against the toilet.

Two quick smacking sounds and Bart shot back past the opening, banging into the next stall hard enough to rattle the walls. Josh could see Bart under the dividing wall, squirming on the floor and crying out in pain.

Josh jumped up and peeked out.

Jones stepped forward and delivered a kick to Bart's stomach with the thud of a punted football. Bart grunted and wretched, then scrambled into the corner, covering his face with his hands, cringing, and sobbing for Jones to stop. Bright ribbons of blood leaked from beneath Bart's hands and dribbled from his chin onto the small, white floor tiles.

Jones loomed over Bart, his fists clenched and raised as if he had no intention of stopping. The veins in his neck bulged like Rocky's. Josh put a hand on Jones's shoulder.

"It's okay," Josh said.

"It's *not* okay," Jones said, directing his snarl at Bart. "You don't touch Josh again. He's twelve, you jerk. You got a problem, you come see me. You don't even *look* at him, you got that?"

Bart nodded and whimpered, but it wasn't enough for Jones, and he shouted, "You got that!"

Jones lunged at Bart, ready to strike.

"Yes!" Bart said, nodding furiously and covering his head, his voice nasal and drowning in blood. "Yes! I got it! Yes. Yes."

Jones let his hands fall to his sides, but he stood

panting and glowering at Bart.

"Not ever," Jones said, stabbing his finger. "Or I'll come looking for you."

"I won't," Bart whined, shaking his head.

"Come on, Jonesy," Josh said, tugging on his teammate's arm and dragging him out of the bathroom.

Jones shook Josh free and said, "I gotta wash my hands. You better wash yours, too."

"What about him?" Josh asked in a whisper, afraid someone would come and they'd be in trouble.

"Forget him," Jones said loudly with disgust, stepping up to the sink and soaping up his hands. "Anyone asks, he slipped."

Josh followed Jones's lead and washed his hands, scrubbing up past his elbows and drying off with paper towels.

Bart stayed in the corner, bleeding and sniffling.

As they marched out of the restroom, Josh thanked his teammate.

"I never liked that guy anyway," Jones said, cracking the knuckles of his fingers one at a time.

"I was gonna hit him," Josh said, feeling suddenly foolish.

Jones looked at him and smiled, "Yeah, well, it looked like he ambushed you."

"He kind of did," Josh said, nodding vigorously.

"So, you got back up, that's all," Jones said. "I'm sure if I wasn't there, you'd have done the same thing to him.

Might have taken you a little longer."

"That's for sure. *Bam. Smack.* And he went flying."

"Yeah," Jones said, rubbing his knuckles. "My older brother used to make me box him in the garage. He's in the marines."

When they arrived at where the team sat eating fries and drinking sodas, Rocky looked up.

"Hey," the coach said. "Jones."

Everyone got quiet and stared at Jones. Josh hadn't even realized it—hadn't looked at anything but Jones's fists and face—but the big first baseman's T-shirt had a brilliant spray of blood down his right side.

"What happened?" Rocky asked.

CHAPTER THIRTY-FOUR

JONES LOOKED DOWN AT the spray of blood on his T-shirt and said, "Nothing, Coach."

"Something," Rocky said, scowling. "You guys okay?"

"It was my fault, Coach," Josh said, stepping forward. "I got into some trouble and Jones, well, he just helped me."

Rocky studied Josh, then returned his attention to the blood, his face still serious and stern.

"We got an important tournament this weekend, and I can't have my starting first baseman breaking his hand in a fight," Rocky said.

"My hand's okay," Jones said, flexing it for the coach.

Rocky looked at him for another couple seconds, then said, "No more fighting. I mean it. Think of the team."

"Okay, Coach," Jones said. "Sorry."

Rocky returned to his fries. Josh got his food from Moose, and he and Jones sat down together next to Tucker and Watson. Both of them hunched over the table and whispered to Jones to tell them what the heck happened. Jones had checked to see that no coaches were listening in before telling them.

"He was messing with our man," Jones said in conclusion. "So . . ."

"You whupped him," Tucker said. "I wish I was there. I hate that smelly creep. Man, look at that blood. I love blood."

Jones stuck a fry in his mouth and looked at Tucker as if he were weird.

"What's that guy dating an eighth grader for, anyway?" Watson said, taking a drink of his soda and shaking his head.

Jones shrugged and said, "No idea, but our man snagged his girl. Things happen."

"I didn't really," Josh said, trying to think of how he could explain the situation with Sheila without sounding stupid but coming up with nothing.

"Sure," Watson said, not believing him anyway.

"Don't worry, junior," Tucker said to Josh, "we got you covered. Ain't no high school kid gonna mess with our shortstop. I don't care who he is. You go ahead and date anyone you like, except my sister."

"Your sister has bigger calves than you," Jones said.

"Don't talk about my sister," Tucker said, crumpling a napkin and bouncing it off of Jones's forehead.

"Easy, big guy. I'm just saying," Jones said, drinking his soda.

"So, junior Josh is really one of us, isn't he?" Tucker asked. "Diapers and all?"

Jones raised an eyebrow at Tucker and said, "You're the one who picked him up and paraded him around."

"I know. I'm saying it nice," Tucker said.

"Oh," Jones said, popping another fry in his mouth.

"And, I'm saying that if he's one of us," Tucker said, lowering his voice and leaning across the table again, "shouldn't we cut him in on the gym candy?"

Jones looked away, shaking his head.

"What?" Tucker said. "He can use it."

"What candy?" Josh asked.

"You want to win games, right?" Tucker asked.

"Of course," Josh said.

"We do what we have to to win, right?" Tucker asked.

"We work harder than anyone," Josh said.

"Exactly," Tucker said, jabbing a finger at Josh. "We win because we work harder. We lift like crazy. We're good, too, but we're stronger than the other teams. That's what the game's about now. Think about it— Bonds, Clemens, McGwire—the great ones are all strong, and gym candy gets you strong."

"Like Super Stax?" Josh asked.

Tucker rolled his eyes. "Listen, you live on the north side, right?"

"On Turtle Street," Josh said, nodding.

"Yeah, I'm over by Schiller Park," Tucker said. "Tell you what; I'll ride my bike over tonight, meet you after dinner in Washington Square Park. I'll hook you up."

Josh looked at Jones for some help, but the towering first baseman put another french fry in his mouth and chewed as he studied the big white column behind their table.

"I guess," Josh said.

"You guess?" Tucker said, scowling. "You on this team or aren't you? My man just drew blood for you. That not enough?"

"Sure," Josh said.

"Good," Tucker said. "Don't say anything to your parents or anything. This is just between us guys. That's how we roll."

"I wouldn't," Josh said.

"Good," Tucker said, winking. "I'll meet you at eight."

CHAPTER THIRTY-FIVE

THE COACHES BROUGHT THE team back to Mount Olympus Sports, where the parents picked them up. Josh said little at dinner. He noticed that his parents seemed to be getting along better but was too distracted about his meeting with Tucker to give it much thought. Sometime during the meal, rain began to clatter against the kitchen window. After dinner Josh helped his mom clean up while Laurel banged her sip cup on her tray and screamed Josh's name, alternating it with the word *peek-a-boo*, meaning she wanted him to play. Normally he would, but when he finished helping, he draped a dish towel over her face just once before disappearing from the kitchen.

Josh pulled on his raincoat and crossed the driveway to the garage, where his father lay with his feet sticking out from under the Taurus.

"What are you doing?" Josh asked him.

"Hand me that wrench over there, will you?" his father asked, wiggling one boot in the general direction of where the wrench lay on the cracked concrete floor.

Josh scooped it up and placed it into the hand that appeared from behind the front tire.

His father grunted and said, "Trying to change the oil."

"Why didn't you take it to the shop?" Josh asked.

His father's legs went still, and the clanking of the wrench stopped. Josh heard him sigh.

"We gotta be a little careful for a while," his father said from under the car before tapping something with the wrench.

"Careful?" Josh said.

"With money," his father said. "It's no big deal. We're okay."

"You don't make as much as you did with baseball?" Josh asked.

"Baseball pays pretty good," his father said, "even Triple-A."

"So it's good you got the job with Rocky," Josh said.

"Real good," his father said. "Most guys leave the game and make a lot less. I'm lucky to have it."

"That's good," Josh said.

Something clunked down onto the concrete floor.

"Oh, crap," his father said. "Hand me that pan

quick, will you, Josh?"

Josh knelt down and slid a metal pan under the car. He heard it scraping along the floor before his father started to worm his way out from underneath. His right hand appeared, smeared black with oil and gripping the edge of the car frame. As he pulled himself out, Josh could see that his father's shirt and face had also been splashed with oil.

"I'm no mechanic," his father said, wiping one eye with the back of his left wrist. "Your mom and I would like to stay here, keep this house. The job with Rocky makes it a lot easier to do it.

"So, aside from me having to do a little mechanical stuff," his father continued, grinning through the spatters of oil, "we're all set. You going someplace?"

"Uh, just to meet a couple of the guys," Josh said. "Nothing big."

His father nodded. "I told you it would all work out. It's raining, though. Still going? Make sure you put your hood up and be back by nine."

"Dad?" Josh said, pulling his hood up and tying it down.

"Yeah?"

"I want to be great at baseball."

"You will be," his father said.

"But it takes a lot of hard work, right?" Josh said.

"And that's what you're doing," his father said. "That's why I've got you on the Titans."

"All that weight lifting," Josh said. "It's important, huh?"

"Size and strength are the difference between what I had and what you're going to have," his father said, his eyes drifting to an old tire that rested against the garage wall.

Josh said nothing.

"Well, I gotta get back under there," his father said, picking up a tool that had a long canvas loop hanging from its end. "I gotta do the filter, too."

"And you have to do whatever it takes, right?" Josh asked before his father could disappear again, underneath the car.

His father lay on his back on the broken floor, and his eyes darted back at Josh. Josh could feel them boring into his brain.

"Whatever it takes," his father said softly. "That's the difference between good and great. You do things to your body other people are afraid to do. You push harder. You do everything Rocky tells you."

Josh realized that he hadn't let go of his last breath and when he finally did, it came out in a long hiss.

"That's what I thought," Josh said, but his father had already disappeared back under the car.

CHAPTER THIRTY-SIX

JOSH POPPED THE KICKSTAND and walked his bike to the garage's open doorway. He flipped his phone out and sent a text message to Tucker. He had to wait only a second before he got a reply that they were still on. His father was banging again under the car, so Josh mounted the bike and pedaled off into the rain and under the dark sky.

Since the sidewalks were broken and bumpy, Josh kept to the streets. When cars hissed past they sprayed him with a fine mist and bled trails of red light along the wet road. Rain pattered down on Josh's hood. Old trees rose up in the dark, standing watch against the ring of battered houses that surrounded the park. Josh rode up the brick walkway in the center, past the Le Moyne Drinking Fountain—a round block of stone with an image of the Jesuit who'd founded Syracuse—the Salt City—carved on its face. He passed by the basketball courts and pulled up under the park's lone, small pavilion.

Imprisoned beneath the rectangular roof were four battered benches, one with a metal trash can chained to its leg. Tucker's ten-speed bike rested against the far bench, and he sat sprawled out on another with both arms extended along the backrest. He wore a green Titans hat turned backward and a bright red rain jacket. His sneakers bubbled and squished when he rocked forward to shake Josh's hand. His hair hung wet and limp and dark like seaweed from under the band of his hat.

"What's up?" Tucker asked, tilting his head up and down as he sat back comfortably.

"Raining pretty good," Josh said, stepping on his kickstand and resting his bike.

Tucker looked around as if it were the first time he noticed the weather. Except for the two of them, the park was as empty, dark, and gloomy as a dirt-floor basement. The streetlights washed over them in a misty glow that reflected dully off the teeth in Tucker's smile.

"Good for a secret meeting," Tucker said. "It *is* secret, right? You didn't tell your parents or anyone or anything, right?"

"No," Josh said. "You said not to."

"Because this is down low," Tucker said. He patted

the bench seat beside him. "Sit."

Josh did, and tried to see what it was that Tucker was looking at. Down the hill, over the rooftops of the murky houses, and across the interstate highway, a red light blinked high above the ground, visible even through the rain.

"Destiny," Tucker said, nodding toward the light.

"The mall?" Josh asked, knowing the Destiny USA mall stood out there somewhere in the gloom and that the light was probably atop its central tower to warn airplanes.

"Destiny," Tucker repeated, as if Josh hadn't spoken.

Tucker reached into his rain jacket pocket and removed an amber vial with a white plastic cap. A pill bottle, just like you'd get from a doctor. He twisted off the lid and shook a pill into Josh's hand. The smooth white lozenge bore an imprint that read A17.

"Gym candy," Tucker said. "You take one in the morning and one at night, before you eat."

"But what is it?" Josh asked.

"Good for you is what it is," Tucker said. "What? You don't trust me?"

"Yeah, I do," Josh said, giving back the pill.

"You won't believe how strong you're gonna get," Tucker said. "Remember that pop fly you hit against Hempstead? The one in the first inning when we had the bases loaded?"

Josh nodded.

"Three, four weeks from now? That same ball is *gone*," Tucker said. "A home run easy. This stuff is all you need."

"Is it safe?" Josh asked.

Tucker snorted and shook his head. "Does it look like it's doing anything bad to me? How about Watson? How about your boy Jones?"

"Jones?"

"It's a team thing, junior," Tucker said through his teeth.

"And Rocky knows?"

Tucker shook his head. "Too many questions, junior."

"'Cause my dad says I should do whatever Rocky wants," Josh said.

Tucker stared at him for a minute. A jet airplane roared overhead, its blinking lights seeming to be on a crash course with the light atop the Destiny USA tower.

Finally Tucker said, "Yeah, Rocky wants it. Where do you think I got this stuff?"

CHAPTER THIRTY-SEVEN

JOSH GOT ON HIS bike and waved good-bye to Tucker. The bottle of pills rattled in his pocket whenever he hit a pothole or a bump in the street. He looked at his watch and knew he had a little time. Instead of turning off Park Street onto Turtle, he kept going until he got to Pond Street and took a left until he hit the corner of Carbon. While Josh had never been to her house, he remembered Jaden telling his mother the night they had beef stew that she and her father lived on this corner.

He walked up the steps and onto the wide porch of what had once been a fancy white house with gingerbread trim and a round tower in one corner. The peeling paint left it looking shabby, but it was Josh's best bet at where a doctor might live. He knocked, and an old woman wearing glasses yanked open the inside door, washing the porch in a cold, bluish light.

Josh smiled at her, but she waved at him through the glass storm door and shouted, "Go away! I don't want any."

"I'm looking for the Neidermeyers," Josh said loudly. "Doctor Neidermeyer."

The woman scrunched up her wizened face and, pointing, said, "Across the street."

She slammed the door, and Josh retreated to his bike. He rolled it across the street and mounted the concrete steps of a red row house nearly as narrow as his own. From the stoop, he could see through the curtains of the front room and into the living room. Jaden's father sat at a desk, working on a computer. Jaden sat beside him on the couch with her legs curled underneath her, reading a book and stroking an orange-striped cat. Next to her, the light from a lamp burned through its heavy shade to fill the scene with an orange glow.

Josh stuck out a finger and moved it toward the lighted button for the bell but froze only an inch away. His finger trembled. In his mind whirled a series of scenes that could play out, none of them hopeful, all ending with Jaden slamming the door in his face just like the old lady across the street had done. His hand gripped the pill bottle, and the pills rattled inside it. He pushed the button, wincing.

Nothing happened.

Josh thought about what Tucker had said—destiny. If it was his destiny, the doorbell would have worked.

He turned to go but didn't get to the bottom step before he heard the door swing open behind him.

"Hey," a voice said. "Who are you?"

CHAPTER THIRTY-EIGHT

JOSH SPUN AROUND AND stared up at Jaden's father, his eyes peering out from under the hood of a raincoat behind his small, round glasses.

"You're Jaden's friend," her father said.

"Hi, Dr. Neidermeyer," Josh said. "Joshua LeBlanc."

"What are you doing, Josh?"

Josh felt his ears burning. "I was, well, I was going to ring, but I thought it was too late."

Dr. Neidermeyer looked at his watch and said, "A little late, but not a big deal. I'm on my way to Eckerd. My printer ran out of ink. Here, come in. Don't stand in the rain. You can keep Jaden company until I get back."

"Who's keeping me company?" Jaden asked as she peered out from behind her father.

When she saw Josh, she pressed her lips into a flat line.

"I just had to tell you something," Josh said quietly.

Jaden stood beside her father now, with her arms folded across her chest, staring at him.

"Well?" her father said, looking at her.

"He can come in for a minute," Jaden said sullenly.

"I'll be right back," her father said, then stuffed his hands in his pockets and jogged off down the sidewalk in the direction of the drugstore.

Josh watched him go, his sneakers flashing in the rain.

"Well?" Jaden said impatiently, holding the door open.

Josh scooted back up the steps and went in. The warmth of the house seeped into his wet fingers. His eyes seemed to relax in the comfort of the cozy light from the living room. He smelled cinnamon, and something baking.

He sniffed the air and asked, "What's that?"

"Cookies," she said, walking into the living room and plopping back down on the couch. "For my dad."

"Uh, should I take my coat off?" Josh asked.

"I don't know," she said, pasting a fake smile on her face. "That depends on what you have to say and how long it will take to say it."

Josh slipped out of his raincoat and hung it, dripping, from a peg on a rack that held two other coats and several hats on either side of a full-length mirror.

He took a step into the living room, off the wood floor and onto a worn Oriental rug. He cupped the bottle of pills in his hand and stuffed it into the front pocket of his jeans.

"I didn't know which house was yours," he said. "I went across the street. She's kind of a crab."

"That look more like a doctor's house to you?" Jaden asked. "That big white thing?"

Josh shrugged, not wanting to argue.

"My dad had to pay for medical school by himself and support me, too," she said, sounding angry. "Instead of doing what most doctors do, he's spent his time as a resident doing free clinics for poor people. So, he doesn't get to drive a Porsche, like your coach, and we live here."

"It's nice," Josh said, looking around. "As nice as my house."

Jaden's face softened a little and she picked up the cat.

"I wanted to say I'm sorry," Josh said.

Her face softened even more. Her cheeks flushed and she looked down.

"That's okay," she muttered. "I'm kind of sorry, too. It's just that I write that article about you and the team, and everyone was giving me grief about it anyway, and then you leave and your dad takes Esch away and now we stink again, and everyone says you're going out with Sheila, and I look like a jerk."

"You don't look like a jerk," Josh said, sitting down

on the big chair facing the couch.

She looked up at him and said, "I want to win a Pulitzer Prize. That's my goal."

"Why can't you?" Josh asked. "You're smart."

She shook her head and said, "You can't get there by writing things for yourself. You have to have integrity, write things the way they really are, not the way you want them to be."

"What's that got to do with me playing for the Titans?" Josh asked, afraid he sounded stupid.

Jaden looked up to the ceiling, then back at him, and said, "I wrote that article, yes, because you are a great player, but also because I *like* you."

Josh shifted in his seat and cleared his throat. Jaden hung her head and stroked the cat.

"I like you, too," Josh said.

CHAPTER THIRTY-NINE

WHEN JADEN LOOKED UP, Josh could see that her eyes swam in tears, even though none spilled down her cheeks.

"But you're with *her*," Jaden said.

Josh shook his head violently. "I'm *not*. That's the crazy thing. I didn't say anything. She just sat down at lunch and asked me out, and I didn't say anything, and Benji, he started telling everyone, and she did, too, I guess, but I'm not."

Jaden looked at him, and the sad expression on her face began to melt away, replaced by the glow of a small smile.

"Well, that's good," Jaden said.

"This whole 'going out' thing," Josh said. "It's all crazy. I don't even know what it means. There, I said it. I'm stupid."

"You're not stupid," Jaden said.

"People say they're going out, and I don't see what that means," Josh said.

"Just that they like each other," Jaden said. "It doesn't have to mean more than that."

"What about kissing and all that?" Josh said, looking away from her, his cheeks on fire now along with his ears.

"People can do that if they want," she said. "They don't have to if they don't. It's just a way of saying you like each other, that's all."

"So?" Josh said.

Jaden got up and rounded the coffee table. Josh kept his head down, but he looked up with his eyes. She bent down and gently kissed his cheek.

"So," she said, then sat back down on the couch, grinning now.

Josh grinned back and shrugged. "That's not a big deal, right?"

Jaden shook her head and said, "Not really."

"And we're going out?" Josh said.

"Does it matter?" Jaden asked.

Josh shook his head and said, "Benji says you should text a girl every day."

"I like to get text messages," Jaden said. "But what does Benji know about going out with girls?"

"Nothing, really," Josh said.

"Right," she said, picking up the cat. "We like each

other. That's all for now. We just see what happens."

"That sounds pretty smart," Josh said. "You're smart. That's why I wanted to talk to you."

"Not so that I would kiss you?" she asked.

"No," he said, looking down.

"Don't worry," she said. "I'm kidding."

"This can be just between us, right?" Josh asked.

"Of course," Jaden said.

Josh nodded and removed the bottle of pills from his pants pocket, holding it up in the warm orange light, rattling it gently.

"This is what I wanted to ask you about," he said.

"Here, Mittens, sit down," Jaden said, setting the cat on a cushion and reaching for the bottle. "What is it?"

"That's what I want you to tell me," he said.

She examined the bottle and said, "It looks like prescription drugs, but there's no label. It could be anything."

"You ever heard of gym candy?" Josh asked.

Jaden narrowed her eyes and said, "Steroids?"

Josh shrugged. "That's what I wondered."

Jaden twisted off the top and shook a pill out into her palm, studying the markings before putting them back.

"That's what they call steroids—gym candy," she said. "But that doesn't mean this is that."

"Someone told me it was gym candy," Josh said.

Jaden studied him and asked, "Someone you trust?"

"I don't know," Josh said, wrinkling his brow.

"How could you, right?" she said. "If they're telling the truth, how can you trust them? Who'd give a kid—no offense, I'm a kid too—who'd give a kid steroids? No one you can trust."

"And if it's not really steroids or gym candy or whatever you call it," Josh said, "then they lied to begin with."

"That's what I mean," Jaden said.

"I told you you were smart."

"So," Jaden said, "what do you want me to do?"

"Find out what they really are," Josh said. "Remember the night I walked you to the hospital to meet your dad?"

"Yes."

"Remember I said that Porsche looked like Rocky Valentine's but I said, why would he be there?" Josh asked.

"Yes."

"Well," Josh said, "I never told you because your dad came, but it *was* his car. The license plate said DOIT2IT. That's his saying, 'Do it to it.' So, I'm riding over here tonight and I'm thinking, if this stuff *is* coming from Rocky but it's really a drug you need to get from a doctor, well . . ."

"He's getting it from a doctor at the hospital?" Jaden said.

"Maybe," Josh said. "What do you think?"

"Forget what I think," she said. "The question is, what would a good reporter do?"

Josh shrugged.

"A good reporter first finds out what this is," Jaden said, shaking the bottle and rattling the pills again as she handed the bottle back to him. "Once we do that, we find out where it came from. If it really is steroids, we have to tell someone."

"Like our parents?" Josh said, wincing and sucking in air through his teeth as he stuffed the bottle back into his pants pocket.

Jaden pressed her lips tight and shook her head.

"No," she said, "like the police."

CHAPTER FORTY

JOSH STARED AT HER. Mittens hopped down onto the floor with a light thud and walked out of the room, swishing its tail. An old wooden clock on the wall ticked with a small sound like spit bubbles popping.

"You can't," Josh said. "You promised. This is between us. You said."

"But Josh," she said, "this is dangerous. This is illegal."

"You promised," Josh said, scowling at her.

"I know, I know," she said, raising a hand in the air. "But why? Why wouldn't you want to stop this?"

Josh sat looking at his own hands, squeezing them into fists, then letting them relax, then squeezing them again as if he could extract his worry the way a farmer milks a cow.

171

"My father," Josh said in barely a whisper.

"Your father is in on this?" Jaden asked with shock.

Josh shook his head. "No, but he works for Rocky. He's doing well. I don't want any trouble for Rocky. I don't want trouble for my dad. This retiring thing. Don't say anything, but he got cut from the team. They let him go. Baseball was my dad's life."

"A first-round pick out of high school," Jaden said with a nod.

"I know," Josh said. "Now it's gone, and this job is all he's got."

"He's got you and your mom and your sister," Jaden said.

"But outside that," Josh said, "this job with Rocky? That's it."

Jaden looked at him for a moment and sighed before she said, "Josh, do you know how dangerous this stuff is if it is steroids?"

"No, I guess not."

"Forget about the mood swings and acne," Jaden said. "This stuff can *kill* you. Liver damage. Kidney damage. Heart damage. In teenagers, it sometimes stops their growth completely. This is so illegal, Josh. For him to be doing that."

"If he is," Josh said.

"Right," Jaden said. "But if he is, we have to stop it."

"But we have to stop it *without* the police," Josh said. "This is my secret. I told you when you promised that it was between us. You can't go back on that."

Jaden shook her head. "You're right, I can't."

"Then we do this my way," Josh said. "First we do what you said—we find out if it's real. Who knows? This could be a placebo."

Jaden twisted her lips and said, "What? He's supposedly giving out steroids, but they're really not?"

"You said yourself that they give people sugar pills and the people get stronger just because they think they're taking steroids," Josh said. "Or maybe it's just another supplement and Tucker is telling me it's gym candy just to mess with me. It's possible."

"I guess," Jaden said. "I doubt it, but you're right, we have to find out."

"Can you do that?" Josh asked. "I don't want you asking your dad."

Jaden thought for a moment, then said, "The *PDR*—my dad has one."

"What's that?"

"*Physicians' Desk Reference*," Jaden said, getting up from the couch and reaching for the shelf above her dad's desk.

Jaden removed a red book, thicker and heavier than a phone book. She laid it down in front of him on the coffee table and flipped it open to one of the pages toward the front. Small, rectangular photos made a grid filling the page.

"See this?" Jaden said, pointing to the picture of two

yellow, oval pills with ZX1 stamped on them. "It's an index."

"It has every pill made?" Josh asked.

"Except for some of the generic stuff," Jaden said. "But just about everything is in here. Every pill has its own design and markings."

Josh flipped a couple pages and said, "There must be thousands."

"Yup," Jaden said. "You leave me one of those pills. It might take a little time, but I'll find out what it is."

Josh looked at the front door.

"Don't worry," she said. "I'll take it up to my room and he'll never know it's gone."

"I've got to go, anyway," Josh said, taking a look at the clock and dropping a pill into her outstretched hand.

"Who knows?" Jaden said, closing her hand. "Maybe I'll have news for you tomorrow in school."

"If you find out tonight," Josh said, pulling on his raincoat and sticking the pill bottle in the side pocket, "send me a text."

"Even if it's late?"

"I'll put my phone on vibrate. If I'm awake, I'll get it," Josh said. "And tomorrow? You want to sit with me at lunch?"

Jaden smiled. She closed the book, took a step toward the stairs, and said, "That'll set Sheila straight."

"And you won't say anything to anyone about all this?" Josh asked.

"If these are steroids," Jaden said, opening her hand so the pill rested in the center of her palm, "I won't stop trying to convince you we should tell the police, but I'm not going to do it unless you say it's okay. I made a promise, and I keep my promises."

"Thanks, Jaden," Josh said, putting his hand on her arm and giving it a gentle squeeze. "I knew I could count on you."

"Okay," Jaden said, closing her hand around the pill, "I better get this upstairs."

Before she took another step, the latch on the front door rattled and Jaden's father burst into the room. In his hand he carried a small orange plastic bag from the drugstore. The hand in which Jaden held the pill disappeared behind her back.

"Jaden?" her father said. "What are you doing?"

CHAPTER FORTY-ONE

"DAD," JADEN SAID. "HI."

"Hi, Dr. Neidermeyer," Josh said, his mind spinning fast and latching on to an idea. "We've got this science fair project coming up, and I asked Jaden to give me some help with it."

"With my *PDR*?" her dad said.

"Uh, I know from my dad playing baseball for so long that they use a lot of anti-inflammatory pills in sports," Josh said, sweat breaking out on his upper lip. "So I wanted to make a poster of the different kinds and I, uh, wanted to have pictures of the different pills, and Jaden said she could get me some ideas from that book."

Her father studied him for a few seconds through his foggy, rain-spattered glasses before he said, "That's the right book then."

Dr. Neidermeyer shed his raincoat and sneakers, then crossed the room and knelt down in front of the printer that was tucked under his desk, back to his own business.

"So, okay," Josh said in a loud, robotic voice her father could hear, "thanks, Jaden. See you in school."

"See you," Jaden said, waving a limp hand and wearing a pained look on her face as if it hurt her to lie.

Josh left and climbed on his bike but didn't get past the first telephone pole before his phone buzzed. He fished the phone out of his pants pocket and flipped it open without stopping the bike.

"THAT WAS 2 CLOSE," Jaden said in her text.

Josh nodded as if she could see him. He snapped the phone shut, buried it deep in his pants pocket to stay dry, gripped his handlebars, and raised his backside up off the bike seat, pedaling hard for home.

By the time Josh arrived, his father had finished the oil job in the garage and gotten cleaned up. He sat on the couch in the living room beside Josh's mom, watching a Yankees game.

"You're soaked," his mom said, standing up and wringing her hands. "Get into the shower, Josh."

"And you're late," his father said, glancing at his watch but returning his attention to the TV immediately.

"Let me take your coat," his mom said, stepping into the kitchen and reaching for his coat.

"No, that's okay," Josh said, retreating into the little

open closet area beside the door where their coats hung on hooks in the wall. "I got it."

Josh slipped the pill bottle out of the raincoat and into his pants pocket.

"What's that?" his mother asked.

Josh whirled around, his face hot. "Nothing."

His fingers did a quick switch inside his pocket, and he took out the phone.

"Just my phone," he said.

"Why's your face red?" his mom asked.

Josh wagged his head, looking down at his feet and kicking off the wet sneakers.

"It's a text message from Jaden," he said. "That's all."

"Jaden?" his mom said. "You two are texting each other now?"

"Mom. Stop."

His mother turned away, raising her hands in the air. "I'm just asking. I think she's nice."

"She is," Josh said.

"You better go get a hot shower," his mom said, complaining. "Riding your bike around in the rain."

"I had to meet the guys," Josh said. "I got my homework done in study hall."

"Lights out at nine-thirty," his mom said. "That's twenty minutes."

"Can't I read?" Josh asked.

"Okay," his mom said, returning to the couch in the other room. "Just until ten, and be quiet up there so you don't wake your sister."

Josh kissed his parents and went upstairs to get ready for bed. As he returned his toothbrush to its place in the ceramic mug beside the sink, his cell phone buzzed and vibrated across the top of the toilet tank, sounding like a jackhammer. He snatched it up and popped it open, expecting a text but hearing Benji's voice instead.

"Hey," Benji said. "You forget your main man?"

"What?" Josh said.

"You said you'd call me with the answer to problem thirty-two in the math," Benji said. "Remember?"

"Oh, yeah," Josh said. "I forgot."

"Dude, you need to eat some fish."

"Fish?"

"Helps your brain," Benji said. "My mom makes fish every Tuesday night. The whole house smells like a sewer, but we're one sharp bunch."

"Then why do you need me for problem thirty-two?" Josh asked, whispering as he crossed the hall into his room, where he quietly closed the door.

"Stop flattering yourself," Benji said. "You're genetically predisposed to math and I'm not."

"Genetically predisposed?" Josh said, wrinkling his face and looking at the phone.

"See?" Benji said. "Science. Genetics. That's where I rule and you drool."

"Cool," Josh said, tucking the phone under his chin so he could talk while he changed into a clean

T-shirt and boxers.

"So, give me the goods," Benji said.

Josh finished changing, then dug his math book out of his backpack and removed the homework sheet, reading off the steps to Benji.

"Super," Benji said. "Hey, did you text Sheila? Girls like to get text messages, especially at night. I figured I should remind you since girls are like science to you."

"Forget Sheila," Josh said, putting away the math, grabbing his book, and sliding into bed.

"Dude, my hearing must be haywire. I know you didn't just say forget the goddess of Grant Middle."

"Forget her," Josh said. "I gotta go. Talk to you tomorrow."

Before Benji could reply, Josh ended the call and opened his book. Before he started to read, he sent a text to Jaden that said "ANYTHING YET?"

A minute later, the phone buzzed and he opened it for the reply.

"NO."

Josh sighed and found his place in the book, losing himself in it and forgetting for a time about Rocky and Tucker and steroids and girls. At ten his mom popped her head in and, yawning, told him to turn off the light. Josh stashed the phone underneath his pillow, checking it one final time before he closed his eyes.

He was just beginning to drift off when the phone buzzed under the pillow like a wet hornet.

CHAPTER FORTY-TWO

"JADEN?" JOSH SAID, ANSWERING the phone and seeing that it wasn't a text.

"Josh," she said in a whisper, "I didn't want to send a text. It *is* steroids. Anadrol-17—an anabolic steroid. My God, this is insane."

Josh's heart raced inside his chest. He bolted up out of bed and bumped his head on the slope of the ceiling.

"Ow!"

"Are you okay?"

"Hit my head," he said, rubbing it and sitting down on the edge of the bed. "I'm fine."

In the glow from the cell phone, he could see the dull glimmer of the Titans trophy on his dresser. His stomach tightened.

"What are we going to do?" Jaden asked, hissing.

"Nothing," Josh said. "Not now."

"We have to tell."

"No," Josh said. "Not that. We have to figure a way to stop him from doing it, but we can't tell. I told you that."

"And I told you I wasn't going to stop trying to convince you," she said. "My dad's coming! I'll see you tomorrow."

The phone went dead. Josh stared at the numbers to convince himself that it hadn't been a dream. Finally he closed the phone and stashed it back under his pillow.

The night ran long, with sleep eluding him like an inside curveball. When he finally did nod off, his dreams were plagued with angry wasps, dark, empty locker rooms, and dugouts filled with pill-popping baseball players whose faces looked like monster fish. The hallway was still dark when Josh slipped across it and into the bathroom to get ready for school.

He huddled with Jaden on the bus, the two of them arguing in whispers back and forth, listening to each other's ideas and coming up with no real plan. During classes, Josh had a hard time listening, and he forgot all about Sheila until she sat down next to him at lunch.

Jaden hadn't arrived yet. Benji sat across the table from them, already munching on a peanut butter and jelly sandwich and washing it down with a carton of milk.

"Oh, I'm sorry, that seat is saved," Josh said.

Sheila looked at him, smiling uncertainly and waiting for the punch line to the joke.

"For Jaden," Josh said, quiet but firm.

Sheila's pretty face turned nasty. She stood fast, and her chair screeched across the floor.

"You think I'm putting up with this?" she asked. "You think I need you?"

"No," Josh said.

"I *don't*," she said.

"Okay," Josh said softly.

"Ha!" Benji cried out through a glob of half-chewed PBJ. "Girl, goddess or not . . ."

Benji wiggled his neck so that his head bopped back and forth like a cobra. "You just got *served*!"

Sheila clamped her lips tight, and her face turned red enough to explode.

"You toad!" she said. She snatched up Benji's milk and dumped it on his head. Then she spun and walked away while the kids around them burst out in a mixture of cheers and jeers.

Benji blinked his eyes and sputtered and wiped them clear with his hands. Milk soaked his hair and discolored the Red Sox T-shirt he wore with a slow-growing dark stain.

"Man," Benji said, looking down at his shirt, "what is it with girls and dumping food on me?"

Jaden walked up, trying not to giggle, and said,

"Because you look so hungry?"

"Funny," Benji said, wiping his face with his hands.

Benji sat looking at them as if someone hadn't just dumped milk all over him. The cafeteria returned to normal, with the drone of everyone talking at the same time adding a buzz to the air. Josh stood and pushed Jaden's chair in for her as she sat down.

Benji stuffed another bite of sandwich into his mouth and said, "Dude, you are so lame. Helping her with her chair? You're like my grandfather."

"There's nothing wrong with nice manners," Jaden said.

Benji rolled his eyes.

"Did you tell him?" Jaden asked.

"Tell me what?" Benji said, leaning across the table.

"Are you crazy?" Josh said to Jaden.

CHAPTER FORTY-THREE

"CRAZY?" BENJI SAID, OUTRAGED. "You're the crazy one. Dude, that is so wrong. I'm your best friend. You don't have secrets from your best friend."

"You weren't my best friend after I left for the Titans," Josh said, taking out a turkey sandwich and biting into it.

"What?" Benji said, widening his eyes.

"The day you dug my oatmeal cookies out of the trash?" Josh said, chewing with his mouth half full.

Benji swatted his hand at the air. "Dude, I was teaching you to respect the friendship, let you know how good of friends we really are. Now, what's she talking about that you didn't tell me?"

Josh scowled at Jaden. She shrugged apologetically. Josh took a drink of milk, then sighed.

"All right," he said, leaning close and whispering. "Rocky's dealing steroids."

"Are you kidding me?" Benji said in a voice loud enough to draw stares.

Josh rolled his eyes, shot Jaden an angry look, and said, "See?"

"Sorry. Sorry," Benji said. "I'm quiet. I'm all quiet now. They don't call me Johnny Tight-lips for nothing."

"Who calls you Johnny Tight-lips?" Josh asked, wrinkling his face.

"No matter," Benji said, holding his hand up like a traffic cop. "Tell me the deal. Are we calling the cops?"

"No!" Josh said, grabbing a handful of Benji's soaked T-shirt, pulling him even closer, and whispering. "We are *not* calling the police or anyone else."

Josh looked over at Jaden and asked, "Did you put him up to this?"

Jaden shook her head and said, "Not me. I didn't say anything."

"Dude," Benji said, removing Josh's hand from his shirt, "the merchandise, go easy."

"I want to stop him, and we will if we can, but we *can't* call the police," Josh said.

"Josh doesn't want his dad to lose his job," Jaden said.

"*He's* dealing, too?" Benji said.

"*No!*" Josh said. "My dad's not dealing. He's got nothing to do with this."

Josh explained the whole situation while trying to eat, not because he was all that hungry, but because he knew he'd need his energy for practice.

When Josh finished, Benji said, "First, you need a sting. You get the goods on him, then you call him and tell him you'll bust him if he doesn't stop. The dude will quit selling the juice before you get off the phone if you sting him."

"Sting?" Josh said.

"Like cops," Benji said, "when they go after someone. They set them up in a *sting*. They offer to buy drugs and put the whole thing on video from one of these cameras you can stick in a little nail hole in the wall. I saw it on *America's Most Wanted*."

"Well, we can't ask him to buy drugs," Josh said. "He's not selling these things on the street. He's just giving them to his team. And we don't have a camera you can stick in a nail hole."

"What's in all this for him?" Benji asked. "Why would he do this?"

"Money. My dad says Rocky has a sponsor package from Nike that might happen that's worth hundreds of thousands of dollars," Josh said, "but they only do it for the top teams in the country. So if the team is great, he makes some pretty big money."

"What if we get him doing the buying?" Jaden asked.

Josh stared at her.

"At the hospital," Jaden said, and she told Benji how they'd seen Rocky's car outside the loading dock.

"So, we need a stakeout," Benji said, wadding up his sandwich wrapper and stuffing it into his lunch bag.

"And we take a picture of the deal going down with a cell phone."

"My cell phone doesn't have a camera," Josh said.

"Mine does," Jaden said.

"Mine, too," Benji said. "Dude, you gotta get into the twenty-first century."

Josh shrugged.

"Anyway," Benji said, "we stake out the loading dock, wait for Rocky to come get the drop, take a picture of the exchange, and run like H-E-double hockey sticks."

"Then we call him anonymously," Jaden said, "and tell him if he keeps doing it, we'll send the picture to the *New York Times*."

"What about the Syracuse paper?" Josh asked.

"Think big, dude," Benji said. "That's how you get the really big bad guys. You gotta think big."

"When do we start?" Josh asked.

"Tonight," Jaden said. "Why wait?"

"I got my fantasy baseball draft tonight," Benji said, "so I'm out."

"We'll take turns," Jaden said. "I'll go first. Can you do tomorrow night? Tomorrow I've got to finish the paper and print it, so I'll be at school until late."

"I got you tomorrow," Benji said.

"I'll help," Josh said. "I mean, I'll go with you both."

They finished their lunch and kept discussing the plan. When the bell rang, Jaden gave Josh a pat on the back and said, "I'll see you tonight."

CHAPTER FORTY-FOUR

WHEN HIS DAD PICKED him up for practice after school, Josh waited until they were halfway there before he asked, "Dad, how's that Nike deal working out?"

His father gave him a quick glance and, scowling, said, "Did your mother tell you? I asked her not to say anything."

"She didn't say anything," Josh said. "I was just talking about it at lunch with my friends."

"I don't want to give it a jinx," Josh's dad said, "but it looks like it's going to happen. They're going to have someone watching practice today."

Josh beamed at his dad and said, "That's great. How come you don't look happy?"

His dad smiled, fought it back, then gave up and smiled again, shaking his head.

"It's just like it's almost too good to be true," his dad said. "When I got let go . . . well, it was like something inside me died, Josh. It's hard to explain. I played base-ball my whole life. It practically was my life, and I really didn't know if I was ever going to be happy doing any-thing again. Now this. It's still baseball; not playing, but everything I know about the game still matters. I just don't want to give it a jinx."

"Being happy won't jinx it," Josh said. "I'm glad I know."

"Why'd you say it like that?" his father asked.

"Like what?" Josh said, part of him wanting to cry out that he wouldn't let the whole thing with Rocky ruin his father's dream.

"Like you can help make it happen?" his father said.

Josh pressed his lips together, then said, "I'm just happy, Dad. That's all. Maybe by doing good today I can help, right?"

"Sounds good," his father said, pulling into the sports complex. "You go work hard. I've got a meeting at the vitamin store for Rocky."

"You're not meeting the Nike guys?" Josh asked.

His father forced a smile and said, "That's not my place yet. This is still Rocky's deal. But I'll be back to pick you up after practice."

Josh changed into his workout clothes and hit the weight room.

As he finished a set of shoulder presses, Tucker sidled up to him and asked, "How you feeling?"

"Still sore from yesterday," Josh said, massaging his legs.

"It'll take a few weeks," Tucker said, lowering his voice but grinning big. "Then, *whoosh*. I told you, you'll take off like a rocket."

Tucker gave him a friendly punch on the shoulder along with a wink before he stalked away.

At practice, Josh saw Rocky on the side, talking and joking with a man wearing a gold watch and a blue Nike sweat suit. But it was also Rocky who stopped practice, pulled on a glove, and walked out onto the field to instruct Josh on the way to drag his right foot across the bag on a double play.

"Look," Rocky said, stepping toward first with his left foot as he caught the ball Moose threw to him, then dragging the right foot across the bag as he threw it to first. "You make tagging the bag just part of the throw. It saves half a second, and that's the difference between one out or making the double play. You try it."

Josh looked over at the Nike guy and bit his lip. He wanted to ask Rocky why he was all of a sudden giving tips out on the field when all he usually cared about was Super Stax and gym candy. Of course, he kept his mouth shut and did as Rocky told him.

On the very next try, Rocky's technique worked. Moose hit a grounder to the second baseman. Josh darted for the bag. The second baseman fumbled the scoop, and the ball came late. Josh snagged the ball, dragged his foot, and rocketed the ball to first, beating the runner by a step.

Rocky stood with his thick arms folded across his chest, grinning. The Nike guy gave a low whistle, and Jonesy pulled his hand free from the glove, shaking it from the sting.

"Now, that's the way you play shortstop," the Nike guy said.

"You mean, that's the way you coach a shortstop," Rocky said, patting the Nike guy on the back until he returned Rocky's grin.

Josh walked back to his position, wondering if tonight would be the night he and Jaden wiped that grin right off of Rocky's face.

CHAPTER FORTY-FIVE

DURING DINNER LATER THAT evening, Josh's father asked, "You take your Super Stax?"

"Not yet," Josh said.

"What's wrong?" his father asked. "You don't like that banana, right?"

"No, it's okay," Josh said.

"Well, take it," his father said. "You need to take that stuff, Josh. You need every edge you can get. We talked about that. You look tired."

"He's wearing himself out," Josh's mom said. "He'll get to bed early tonight."

"No!" Josh said, raising his voice more than he meant to and drawing stares from both his parents.

Laurel banged her sip cup on her tray and shouted, "No. No! No! No!"

"That's enough," his mom said, reaching for his little sister.

"I just have a science project tonight I have to work on with Jaden, that's all," Josh said.

"Science?" his dad said. "I've never seen so much science. What are they trying to do? Put a man on Mars?"

"Genetic predispositions," Josh said.

"It's all the state testing," his mom said to his dad.

His dad grumbled and took a bite of pot roast before attacking his pile of mashed potatoes and gravy, then abruptly pushing back from the table and disappearing upstairs, mumbling something about the bathroom.

"Just try to get done early," his mom told him, getting up from the table and going to the counter where the can of Super Stax rested. "Here, I'll mix in some vanilla and it'll taste better."

"Gee, Mom," Josh said in a soft voice, "you're in on this, too? Do you really care about all this weight-lifting stuff?"

"It's important to your father, Josh," she said, dumping a scoop of the powder into a big glass.

After dinner, Josh helped clean up, then wheeled his bike out of the garage and headed for the hospital. He sent Jaden a text to let her know he was on his way, and she met him on a corner two blocks away from the hospital. The orange sun behind him stretched his shadow for nearly a block. Even though the evening started out warm enough, the shadows had a bite to them that made him think he should have worn more than just his navy blue Syracuse University sweatshirt and jeans. When he saw that Jaden was wearing a jeans jacket over her black hooded sweatshirt, he shivered, wishing he had worn one, too. She waved at him and swung the backpack off her shoulder. When Josh got down off his bike, she unzipped the backpack and removed the big red *PDR*.

"I marked the page," she said, touching a sticky note and flipping open the book. "Wanted you to see for yourself."

Josh followed Jaden's finger down the page to a picture of a pill that looked exactly like the ones Tucker had given him.

"Anadrol-17," he said, reading it aloud, studying the picture. "That's it."

"And here," Jaden said, flipping to another section in the book and showing him where it said that Anadrol-17 was an anabolic steroid.

"I believed you," Josh said.

"I know," she said. "But sometimes I have a hard time believing it myself. I mean, this is the kind of stuff you read about but don't think people would actually do."

"What about all those pro players?" Josh asked.

"Right," she said. "Then you think, but that's the pros. We're talking fourteen-year-olds. So I did some research after school. Four percent of high school kids use steroids. You think, not a big number, right? Until you know that there's sixteen and a half million high school kids. That's more than half a million kids in this country using steroids. It makes the number of pro players look like a raindrop in Onondaga Lake."

Josh held her gaze until she said, "Come on, let's go see if tonight's the night."

CHAPTER FORTY-SIX

JOSH LOOKED AT HIS watch—it was just after seven—and asked, "You think it will be?"

"I was thinking about the last time," Jaden said, beginning to walk. "There's a shift change at eight. That's probably why he was here then. Whoever's supplying him probably gets off the same time as my dad. Also, that day was a Thursday and it's Thursday today, so I think we've got a chance. If Coach Valentine is giving steroids to the whole team, he probably has to get more every week."

Josh tucked his bike behind a ragged patch of bushes next to the sidewalk, and they began their mission. Small houses stood cramped along the street, lurking, aged and sullen, behind withering trees, and half-shaded windows. Josh and Jaden turned the corner and scoped out the loading dock from across the street, walking down the hill and past the concrete cave without stopping until they got to the next corner.

"Where should we wait?" Josh asked. "Behind the Dumpsters?"

"It won't smell good," Jaden said, "but I think it's the only place that's safe. Let's go in one at a time in case there's a security guard around or something. I'll go first."

"I should go," Josh said, taking hold of her shoulder. "If there's no place to hide and something goes wrong, I don't want you to get in trouble."

"I know the docks better than you," she said, slipping free, "and if anything happens, I can just say I'm there to meet my dad."

"What happens if Rocky's there and your dad really comes out?" Josh asked.

"Don't worry," she said. "I told my dad I couldn't meet him tonight, that I'd be at the library. I can stay and see what happens with Rocky if he's here and then get home after my dad."

"I keep saying you're smart."

Jaden touched his hand, smiling, and said, "So, I'll go. When I get set, I'll text you. Hoods up."

Jaden flipped up her hood, hiding her face and hair. Josh did the same, then watched her cross the street and climb the hill toward the loading dock. He tensed when a blue van turned the corner and chugged up the hill, slowing to turn into the loading dock area. Jaden barely looked at the van. When she got to the place where the loading area cut into the side of the hill, she took a quick right and, keeping to the edge of the retaining wall, quickly disappeared from sight into the cavelike entrance.

Five minutes seemed like five hours. The van emerged from the dock and chugged on up the hill. Before it disappeared, Josh got Jaden's text: "OK."

Josh crossed the street and followed her path. When he reached the entrance, he took the quick right and walked between a guardrail and the concrete wall that grew higher as the loading area cut deeper into the hillside. The five large Dumpsters still stood in the corner, two with their backs to the loading area and three along the side wall. Josh scanned the area as he crept forward, ducking down when a man in a blue uniform emerged from an open garage door wheeling a big trash can.

As he eased forward, Josh heard the man tossing bags of garbage into one of the Dumpsters by the dock. He finished and wheeled the big can back into the garage and what must be the maintenance area. Then Josh saw Jaden peek her head out from between the second and third Dumpsters along the wall and wave frantically to him. He hurried to where she was, ducking into the dark fissure between the two huge metal containers. The stink of garbage filled his nose.

His heart thumped against his ribs. Jaden grasped his hand and held it tight.

"It's gonna be pitch-black in here in about twenty minutes," Josh said in a whisper. "Are we gonna be able to see anything?"

"Our eyes will adjust," she said, looking ghostly in her dark, hooded sweatshirt.

"What about taking a picture of him getting the drugs?" Josh asked.

Jaden held up her cell phone and said, "It's got a flash."

Josh nodded. Jaden reached into the hatch on the side of the Dumpster they faced and removed a flattened cardboard box. He followed her as she moved deeper into the space between the Dumpsters, stopping just before they reached the other side. She laid the cardboard down on the slimy blacktop and pointed to it before she sat down herself with her back to the Dumpster. Josh did the same, pulling his knees up tight and using them as a chin rest. From where they sat, they had a perfect view of the loading dock and any cars that pulled in to park.

Josh steadied his breathing and settled in to wait. The shadows lengthened and deepened, and soon everything outside the cones of light from the fixtures dissolved into a murky soup. When the headlights from a car swung across the Dumpsters, they froze. The car rumbled down into the docks and came to a rest amid the handful of other cars parked against the concrete wall. Josh couldn't make out exactly what kind of car it was. He thought it was black, but it could have been dark blue. He knew it wasn't a big car.

The door opened, and someone got out—the shadow of a person too blurred to really see. Then the shape hopped up onto the loading dock and stood briefly under a cone of light before ducking into the shadows of the only open garage door. Josh didn't have to guess anymore.

He had no doubt that the man he saw was Rocky Valentine.

CHAPTER FORTY-SEVEN

JOSH REACHED OUT AND grasped Jaden's hand.

"That's him, right?" Jaden asked in the faintest whisper, her southern accent somehow more pronounced in the dark.

Josh nodded. They stood and pressed themselves against the Dumpster's cool metal side. Josh's fingers played across a thick rib of steel and gripped its edge as though wind from a hurricane might whisk him away. Jaden leaned toward him so that her lips brushed his ear.

"When he gets the drugs," she said in words he had to strain to hear, "I'll jump out and take the picture. Then we run."

Josh nodded but groped for her hand again and tightened his grip to get her attention. He moved his lips to her ear, smelling the strawberry scent of her shampoo, and said, "If they come after us, we'll split up. We'll run down the hill. I'll keep going straight to distract them, and you take a right and head for home. We'll text each other when we're both safe."

Her lips mashed against his ear, making him jump. "You think they'll chase us?"

He could hear the alarm in her voice. He tried to calm his breathing before he said, "No. I'm only saying in case."

Jaden nodded and looked at her watch, pressing a button on the side of it to illuminate the numbers and show him it was just eight. As if on cue, the far door in the opposite corner of the loading dock swung open, stabbing the shadows with a spear of white light that disappeared when it closed. The door began to open and close constantly now as several of the hospital employees left through the back door, the same way Jaden's father did.

As they came out, the bright light behind them made it impossible to see their faces. One by one, they zipped around the closing door and descended the small set of stairs on the far side of the dock. One of them came close and climbed into a car parked along the dock, backing out and zipping away, tires crunching on the gritty pavement.

Josh loosened his grip on Jaden's hand. He leaned in close again to whisper that Rocky might have snuck inside the hospital through the garage door and the maintenance area, but just as his lips brushed her ear, the far door swung open, and the figure that appeared walked right at them, toward the Dumpsters, and away from the stairs where everyone else had gone.

Jaden gripped his hand tight, then let go, removing her camera phone from her jacket pocket and edging toward the loading dock. The door swung shut, cutting off the bright light that kept the figure's face in the shadows, but whoever it was kept close to the garage doors, staying on the fringe of the lights from above. Josh took hold of the Dumpster's corner as Jaden snuck closer, nearly to the edge of the raised loading dock.

The figure moving toward the place where Rocky hid wore a long white lab coat and appeared to have a bag in one hand, although it was so dark Josh couldn't be certain. The sound of footsteps on the concrete came from the black hole of the garage where Rocky had disappeared. Josh saw movement in the shadows, and the figure in the white coat stopped in the darkness in front of another dark shape Josh knew to be Rocky Valentine.

Jaden found a foothold in the loading dock wall, grabbed the edge, and peeked her head over the lip of concrete. She raised her camera phone, and he saw her trying to line up the shapes, knowing she couldn't see much more than he could and that it would be difficult to center the picture.

She'd get only one shot.

Rocky and whoever his supplier was would know that they'd been caught the instant the flash went off. Josh and Jaden would have to run, and if Rocky was as quick as he was strong, they'd have to run fast.

Josh sensed the tension in Jaden's body. He eased out from behind the Dumpsters and into the open space, crouched low and watching but ready to sprint. He could see the two figures talking and Rocky reaching for the bag. Their voices floated across the dark space in low tones. Suddenly Rocky's shape spun toward Jaden.

"Hey!" Rocky shouted.

The camera flash exploded, blasting Rocky and his accomplice with a light so white it blinded Josh. Before he could react, Jaden rocketed past him.

From the pitch-blackness, Rocky screamed with rage.

"Come back here!"

CHAPTER FORTY-EIGHT

JOSH HAD NO IDEA Jaden was that fast. He trailed her hooded shape out of the loading dock, across the street, and down the sidewalk. Her legs flashed like blades on a hedge clipper. Behind him, Rocky kept shouting for them to stop, but that only sent fresh waves of adrenaline through Josh's veins.

When Jaden reached the corner, Josh saw her shoot a quick glance over her shoulder, then break off to the right and down the side street. Josh leaped from the sidewalk without breaking stride, pounding down the pavement in the middle of the street and under a light, where Rocky would be sure not to miss him.

Josh kept going. He risked a quick look back. He saw Rocky reach the spot where Jaden had split off.

Rocky stopped.

Josh slowed and spun around. Rocky swung his head from side to side, deciding which one he should chase.

In a gravelly voice, Josh yelled, "Hey, mister!"

Rocky looked his way.

"Kiss my butt!"

Josh spanked his own backside. Rocky roared and headed right for him. Josh took off, his body numb from panic. After another block, Josh hit State Street, a main thoroughfare. He broke across the street and toward downtown—the opposite way Jaden had gone. Scattered handfuls of young thugs and an occasional bag person provided an obstacle course on the broken sidewalk for Josh to dodge around.

Before he took a left at the next side street, Josh risked a second glance back. He'd gained some distance from Rocky and as Josh turned the corner, he saw the muscle-bound coach bend over and grab at his side, staggering after Josh now with a hitch in his stride. Josh grinned to himself and kept running, going back up the hill and essentially making a big circle before he dashed across the street on which Jaden had turned off. He then ducked down between two parked cars to watch and wait.

After ten minutes, he saw Rocky limping back up the hill on the far side of the street. Five minutes later, he saw the black Porsche speed off, its gears whining with fury. Josh stood up and took the cell phone from his pocket. He'd missed two calls from Jaden. He checked his text messages and wondered why she had called instead of sending a text.

He hit REDIAL and got her on the first ring.

"Oh my God," she said, crying hysterically. "Josh, oh my God."

His heart ached at the sound of her weeping.

"What's wrong?" he said, choking on his words. "Did you get the picture?"

"Yes, come quick," she said, sobbing. "Josh, meet me at the pavilion in Washington Square Park. I can't say it on the phone.

"You're not going to believe who it is."

CHAPTER FORTY-NINE

THE NIGHT HAD ADVANCED far enough to show stars above the whispering treetops and the inky spaghetti strands of the electric wires. Tired as he was, Josh somehow found the energy to jog. On the gloomy side street, he tensed up at the sight of a tall, skinny hooded man bouncing on his toes and heading his way right up the sidewalk. Josh stepped aside at the next driveway, fists ready, but the man passed, sipping on a bottle of whiskey without even looking Josh's way. When he rounded the next corner, Josh scooped his bike up out of the bushes, mounted it, and raced off toward the park. When he saw Jaden slumped on a bench under the shadow of the pavilion, he dumped his bike in the grass and broke into a run.

When he reached her, she threw her arms around

him and clasped him tight, saying his name over and over and crying all the while.

"It's what I deserve," she said bitterly as she withdrew from his arms. "Me and my investigating. Look."

Jaden stabbed at him with her phone. Josh took it and studied the screen. He gasped—a sharp, inward hiss through his front teeth. In the white flash of the photo she'd taken, Rocky Valentine stood taking a bag from the hands of a man in a white lab coat, a man with small, round glasses and a shock of straight dark hair.

The man was Dr. Neidermeyer, Jaden's father.

"Jaden," he said.

"I know," she said, holding up her hand and dropping her chin to her chest. "I'm the one who wanted to go to the police. I'm so ashamed."

"But we don't know—"

"Josh, don't," she said, cutting him off. "We know. You know and I know."

Josh put a hand on her shoulder and squeezed.

"It's okay," he said softly. "You should hear my parents. If they're not in on this, it's only because they don't know about it. It's like everyone is okay with these things. Maybe they're not that dangerous. Your dad's a doctor."

"You think he'd even be a doctor if people knew about this?" she said angrily, flailing her arms in the air. "He'd lose his license in a heartbeat. This stuff isn't okay. This stuff is dangerous. I know that. Everyone knows it."

"People use it, Jaden," Josh said. "No one on the Titans is dropping dead."

"Not yet," Jaden said. "And neither are the people who breathe in a cloud of asbestos. It doesn't kill you instantly. It's not cyanide, but it kills you. You're thirty, forty years old and your liver goes out, or your kidneys, or you have a massive heart attack. Maybe you make it into your fifties or your early sixties, but before it's over, that stuff ends your life sooner than it should."

Josh held out her phone and waited for her to take it back.

"So, what now?" he asked.

"I don't even want to go home," she said, tears filling her eyes afresh. "Everything he said, everything he talks about—how do I know if it's true?"

Jaden leaned against him and Josh held her again. They sat down together on the bench. She buried her face in his chest, and Josh tugged her hood off and ran his hands through the wild thicket of hair that sprang from the band at the back of her head.

Jaden rested her cheek on his shoulder, sighed, and softly said, "He told me my mom died when I was born. They lived in Houston. They weren't even married. He said they couldn't afford a good doctor and after that happened, he decided he'd become one and help people like him and my mom. He said it was for her, what she would have wanted him to do."

"That's nice," Josh said.

"Do you know how proud I was of him?" Jaden said, sitting up and staring fiercely into his eyes. "*Was*. I don't even know if that's what happened. For all I know, my mother didn't want me, or he ran off with me. I have no idea. If he'd lie about this, what wouldn't he lie about?"

Josh gripped her shoulders and said, "Sometimes parents aren't what you think they are, but it doesn't mean they don't love you. Parents are just people. They're just like us."

Jaden shook her head and said, "No, I'm not like that. I'm going to stop him."

"Not the police?" Josh said. "Jaden, you can't."

CHAPTER FIFTY

"**WE'LL STICK TO OUR** plan," Josh said. "We have to. Your dad isn't the only one this would ruin. My dad needs this job. We can stop this thing and everyone can go back to their normal life."

"You think Rocky won't just find another person to get drugs from?" Jaden asked. "You think my father won't sell something else to some other dealer? Maybe it'll be sleeping pills. Maybe painkillers. They're probably safer than that crap."

"I don't know," Josh said. "Maybe you can talk to him."

"I'm not talking to him," Jaden said. "Some doctor. With all those books and his computer and all those crappy papers he writes. It's all a lie."

Josh stood up and took her hand, leading her toward his bike.

"Come on," he said. "I'm going to get you home. It's late. We both need to sleep on this. You ride on the handlebars. I've done it with Benji, so they'll hold you."

Josh pedaled hard through the streets, dropping Jaden at the corner near her house. He gave her a brief hug, patting her back and telling her it would all work out, then headed for home.

"Are you okay?" his mother asked when she saw his face. She was reading a book on the couch while his dad watched something on TV.

"Fine," Josh said. "Just tired."

"Hard work is what wins," his dad said without looking up from the TV.

"Right," Josh said, kissing them both on the forehead and climbing the stairs.

When he got into bed, Josh got a text from Jaden: "IM SO ASHAMED"

He sent her a text right back that said "DONT WORRY. IT WILL ALL B OK"

He jammed the cell phone under his pillow and lay back with his hands behind his head, staring at the slanted ceiling, barely visible in the small amount of light leaking in through the crack at the bottom of his door. The trophy caught his eye, and he studied its foggy shape. He let his mind wander over the situation, thinking about Rocky, the kind of person he was, and what mattered most to him.

It was then that Josh got an idea.

CHAPTER FIFTY-ONE

WHEN JOSH WOKE THE next morning, the idea didn't seem as good as it had in the middle of the night, but he still thought it could work. On the bus, he explained the plan to Jaden.

She looked at him with dull, puffy eyes and said, "Whatever."

"Why do you say that?" Josh asked.

She shrugged and shook her head, then looked out the window.

They rode for a few minutes before Josh said, "You can't just give up."

"I know," she said, her voice flat. "I won't. I'm just tired, Josh. I feel terrible. I can't believe it. My own father."

"Jaden," Josh said. "You don't know what happened. Maybe Rocky threatened him or something."

"With what?" she asked.

"I don't know," Josh said, knowing it sounded ridiculous but wanting to somehow make her feel better. "But if they stop and don't do it again, you have to put this all behind you, forgive and forget. My mom says that's important."

"Your mom's nice," Jaden said, "but I don't know if I can."

"Will you meet me during third period and try my plan?" Josh asked. Josh had study hall for third period, and Jaden had home economics.

"At the dugout?" she asked.

Josh nodded, and Jaden told him she would. The dugout was the only place they could go on school grounds where no one would see them and where they could also get good cell phone reception.

Josh put his books down on the desk in study hall and took out his math homework. He tried to concentrate and get some of it done but found he could do nothing except watch the clock. Ten minutes into the period, he got up and asked for the bathroom pass. Mrs. Grajko handed him the wooden pass without looking up from her work correcting papers.

Josh scooted down the hall, checking behind him before he strolled past the bathroom, jogged down the back stairs, and slipped through the doorway. When he got to the dugout, he found Jaden already there, lying on the bench with her head resting on her backpack.

"Did you just get here?" he asked, peering around the corner to make sure no one had seen or followed him.

Jaden didn't answer; she just shook her head and kept staring up at the wooden slats that held up the roof.

"We said ten minutes into the period, right?" Josh asked, confused.

Jaden sighed, sat up, and said, "What's the difference?"

"You're skipping home ec?" Josh asked.

"Yup."

"You'll get detention," Josh said.

She shrugged and said, "I'll be here until late anyway to get the paper done."

Josh stared at her for a moment, then said, "Well, can we do this?"

"Sure," she said.

Josh took a piece of paper from his pocket and unfolded it. He handed it to her and said, "See? It's not really a script, but I put down the main points during social studies. What do you think?"

Jaden looked at the paper and shrugged.

"Jaden, come on," Josh said. "Snap out of it. We've got to do this. He'd recognize my voice or I'd do it myself. Here, give me your phone. I got his number, and we have to block yours."

Josh punched in *67, then dialed Rocky's cell number

and handed her back the phone.

"You want to rehearse?" he asked.

"No, I got it," she said, hitting the SEND button and putting the phone on speaker so Josh could hear.

"You're anonymous," Josh said. "That's the key, and don't forget the Nike thing. That's huge for him. Big money."

Jaden nodded. The phone rang. Josh's stomach clenched.

Rocky answered, saying hello, his voice rasping with toughness and low like a tuba's. Jaden's eyes widened, and Josh knew Rocky's voice had startled her.

"Uh," she said, "is this Rocky Valentine?"

"Who's this?" he asked in a demanding tone.

"I know about"—Jaden swallowed and looked at Josh's paper—"I know about the steroids."

"Who are *you*?" Rocky asked, nearly shouting the last word.

"I'm the one who took the picture," Jaden said, her voice reverting to her most southern twang so the word came out "pick-chore. "

"I don't know about no picture," Rocky said smoothly.

"I saw you," she said, looking at Josh instead of the paper. "I saw you and my . . . doctor . . . you and Dr. Neidermeyer."

Josh winced.

"'My doctor'?" Rocky said. "So, he's your doctor.

That's how you know about this, huh? Well, I'll have to talk to the good doctor and find out what's going on."

"Don't you dare!" Jaden screamed.

Rocky's guttural laughter sounded like the cough of a sick lawn mower starting up. When he stopped, he said, "Tell you what. You just give me that camera and we forget about this whole thing."

Jaden looked shaken. Josh pointed to his notes on the paper he'd given her and nodded his head.

Jaden looked down and said, "I have the picture on my phone, and it's ready to go. If you don't stop, I'm going to send it to the *New York Times*. What do you think Nike's going to do then?"

Rocky went silent.

"You know about Nike, huh?" Rocky said, almost as if he was pleased and talking to himself. "Okay, I guess you got me. I'll stop and you keep this to yourself, is that it?"

"That's the deal," Jaden said.

Josh nodded and gave her a thumbs-up, then pointed to his eye and then the phone.

"We'll be watching, though," Jaden said.

"Yeah, I bet you will," Rocky said, then hung up.

Josh and Jaden looked at the phone, then at each other.

"What do you think?" Jaden asked.

"I think you did good," Josh said.

"You think he'll stop?" she asked.

"I do," he said.

"Then what's the matter?" she asked. "Why do you look so worried?"

"I don't know," he said. "It's like he knew I was here. Something in his voice just creeped me out, the way he said that about you knowing about Nike."

"I'm sure he didn't know you were here," she said. "How could he?"

"I don't know," Josh said, shrugging. "You're right. It's just something in his voice, and maybe how well I know him. He's a good coach, but he's scary, too. When he looks at you, it's like he sees right through you. Either way, I'll find out soon enough."

"When?"

"Today," Josh said, peering around the edge of the dugout to make sure the coast was clear, "at practice."

CHAPTER FIFTY-TWO

THE YELLOW RUBBER BALLS in the batting cage zipped by Josh like bullets. He blinked and squinted and tried to concentrate, but the only thing he could focus on was the look Rocky gave him at the beginning of practice. The muscular coach didn't say anything, and Josh was sure no one else noticed it, but he also felt sure Rocky had gazed at him a split second longer than normal and that his eyelids had drooped momentarily, like a lizard ready to fall asleep until it suddenly saw something it wanted to eat.

"Get your head out of your behind, LeBlanc!" Moose yelled, feeding another ball into the machine.

Josh swung and dribbled one back at Moose.

"Just lost my groove," Josh said weakly.

Moose grumbled and barked at Josh one more time

at the end before sending him on to the next drill. Jones held the netting aside so Josh could come out of the cage.

"Don't worry, buddy," Jones said. "It happens."

"Thanks, Jonesy," Josh said.

On his way to the ball-toss station in the far corner of the field, Josh watched Rocky striding toward the concrete stairs. Josh checked the stands for his father, thinking that maybe Rocky was going to talk to him about Josh. But Josh's father was nowhere in sight, and instead of talking to any of the parents who sat watching, Rocky disappeared through the main door, which probably meant he was heading to his office.

Josh turned and jogged over to the ball toss. Ten minutes later, Rocky reappeared in the middle of the field and blew the whistle to signal the end of practice. Josh looked up in the stands and waved to his dad, who had just arrived. But either his father didn't see him or something was wrong. Josh's father stood with his hands jammed deep into the pockets of his Windbreaker, his feet spread apart and his neck bulled back, a somber look on his face.

Rocky growled at the team, telling them they'd better improve tomorrow or they might as well not even go to the tournament on Saturday. Moose called them in, and they gave their "Do it to it" cheer and broke for the locker room.

Josh turned to go. When he heard Rocky call his

name in that gruff, raspy voice, Josh's stomach sank like a stone.

He turned and walked slowly toward the coach. Rocky's dark flattop bristles gleamed with hair gel, and his small eyes flickered up and down and around Josh like gnats, without blinking once. Josh's feet scuffed the plastic grass, and the smell of stale sweat filled his nose.

"Yeah, Coach?" Josh asked, swallowing.

"You okay?" Rocky asked, a small smile dancing on his lips.

"Sure," Josh said, blinking.

Rocky held up Moose's clipboard and said, " 'Cause your cage stats stink."

"Just lost my groove," Josh said, the words sounding weak.

Rocky pressed his lips tight, turning his mouth into a hatchet gash. Then, without speaking, Rocky squinted at Josh, nodded, and flicked his chin toward the door, following Josh as he walked.

CHAPTER FIFTY-THREE

JOSH'S STOMACH FLIPPED NOW, rising up, and he hurried for the locker room, where he thought he might lose what was left of his lunch. Instead of trailing him inside, Rocky disappeared, and when Josh passed through the metal doorway, the buzz of talk and the friendly banter of the guys settled his gut. He went straight to his locker, pausing for a second because he thought he'd left it shut but now it was open.

Josh looked around uncertainly. He had presumed the days of the older boys hazing him were long gone. As he removed his clothes, he checked them carefully for signs of Atomic Balm or butter or old chewing gum, but nothing was amiss. Josh forgot about it and even joined in on the banter when Jones loudly asked him who he thought more likely to one day be named to *People* magazine's Sexiest Men Alive list, Jones or Tucker.

Josh voted for Tucker and everyone laughed at Jones, who growled and put Josh in a headlock and gave him a nuggy.

Outside the locker room, Josh found his dad standing off by himself in the lobby, holding his cell phone to one ear and plugging the other one with his free hand so he could hear. Josh's dad was talking business and nodding and explaining something in a tone that sounded too much like pleading for Josh to want to hear, so he waved and pointed to the doors to signal that he'd wait outside. His dad nodded, and Josh found the car and climbed into the front seat, watching the entrance, half expecting Rocky to follow him out.

When his father arrived a couple minutes later, Josh asked, "Everything okay?"

"Sure," his father said, starting the car and pulling away from the curb.

"Because you look kind of mad," Josh said, toying with the zipper on his backpack.

"Hey, I'm sorry," his dad said, brightening. "I'm just trying to close a deal is all. It's nothing to do with you."

"Nothing to do with me and the Titans?" Josh asked.

His dad glanced at him and shook his head. "No, why?"

"I just . . . had a bad day in the batting cage, that's all," Josh said.

"We all do," his dad said, and Josh felt better.

They talked about the Titans' chances in the tournament that weekend and that, because of the last U12 tryouts, his dad would miss the first couple games but would make it for the finals on Sunday. When they got home, Josh's mom asked him to watch Laurel while she put the finishing touches on dinner.

After eating, Josh thought about checking in with Jaden but knew she was working on the school paper and told himself he'd call her when he finished his homework. He was nearly done when his cell phone buzzed and vibrated in his pants pocket. He checked and saw Benji's number.

"What's up?" Josh asked, looking at the time and seeing it was just past eight-thirty, later than he realized.

"How's the paper coming?" Benji asked. "You guys getting anything done, or you too busy kissing?"

"Kissing?" Josh said, glaring at the phone as if Benji could see him. "What are you talking about?"

"You and Jaden," Benji said, making kissing noises into the phone.

"Jaden's at the school," Josh said.

"I know," Benji said, still kissing his phone. "You both are."

"I'm home, meathead," Josh said.

"No you're not," Benji said, without the noises. "She forwarded me the text that you sent to her."

"I just finished math problem forty-seven," Josh said.

"Is that why you called?"

"Dude," Benji said, "why'd you text Jaden that you'd meet her there, then?"

"To do what?" Josh asked.

"I don't know; *you* sent her the text," Benji said. "From earlier."

"Let me go," Josh said. "I'm gonna call her."

"You can't," Benji said. "She's in the school. There's no reception. She took a break outside when she texted me."

"You're teasing me. I didn't send her anything," Josh said, his stomach sinking again.

His phone buzzed and chirped, and he looked at the text Benji forwarded him as they spoke, a text sent from him to Jaden, then from Jaden to Benji.

"ILL MEET U THERE AT 830 LEAVE DA SIDE DOOR OPEN"

"You see that?" Benji asked.

Josh saw that the text had been sent from his phone number, even though it wasn't possible. He punched the menu on his phone and brought up his sent items. The mailbox was empty.

"Someone erased everything," Josh said. "But I never sent that."

"Then who did?" Benji asked. "Who'd want her to think you were going to meet her at the school?"

Josh's mind spun, and it all came together.

"Oh my God," Josh said. "Rocky."

CHAPTER FIFTY-FOUR

JOSH THREW OPEN HIS bedroom door and ran down the stairs, telling Benji to get his bike and meet him at the corner of Grant and Turtle. Josh snapped the phone shut and dashed past the family room, where his parents called out to him from the couch.

"Gotta meet Benji," Josh said without stopping. "Something for school."

"Back by nine-thirty!" his dad shouted after him.

Josh had already snatched his hooded sweatshirt off its hook and was halfway out the door. He flung open the garage door, jumped on his bike, and pedaled like crazy. Streetlights, parked cars, telephone poles, and houses rushed past him in a blur so fast his eyes watered. His legs began to burn; what power he still had left from the grueling practice was beginning to

228

fade. Up ahead, he saw Benji standing beside his bike. Josh zipped past him, leaning into the turn and shooting across the street.

"Come on!" he yelled to Benji, heading up Grant Boulevard toward the school.

After a minute, Benji pulled up alongside him, his face glazed with sweat and pedaling like a madman himself.

"What are we doing?" Benji said.

"It's Rocky," Josh said, puffing. "It's got to be. He took my phone during practice. He must have sent that text, then erased it. He's going to get Jaden."

Benji knew everything from lunch, and he said, "Wait. Josh. We should call the cops."

"And tell them what?" Josh asked, seeing the shape of the school up ahead now, rising in the darkness beyond the streetlights.

"I don't know," Benji said. "That Rocky's going to kill her or something."

"He's not going to kill her," Josh said.

"How do you know?" Benji asked.

Josh didn't answer. He set his teeth and kept pedaling. When he saw a break in traffic, he signaled to Benji. They jumped the curb and shot across Grant and into the school driveway. The office for the school paper was in an unused classroom in the back corner across the hall from the science lab. Tall trees cast dark shadows across the windows and the parking spaces along that side of the school. Two Dumpsters sat slumped like sleeping ogres. Next to them, Josh saw the black Porsche, and he pulled his bike up short.

Benji stopped next to him, breathing hard.

"What do we do?" Benji asked.

Josh climbed off his bike and studied the building. No lights shone from within. But Josh was pretty certain that the room where Jaden should be working on the paper had no outside window.

"Stay here," Josh said, dropping his bike down in the parking lot and heading for the side entrance.

"And do what?" Benji said, his voice breaking with fear.

"I don't know," Josh said. "But if he comes out, don't let him leave."

"What am I supposed to do?" Benji cried, his voice ending in a squeak.

"I don't know. Throw your bike in front of him or something. Just stop him," Josh said, hissing at Benji as he reached for the door handle.

Josh winced at the sound of the hardware groaning and echoing off into the empty school as the door swung open. He kept going, though, and stepped into the barren entryway, his breathing short and fast, his heart hammering away. He tried to listen but heard nothing over the sound of his own breath. Slowly, he climbed the small set of stairs and tiptoed into the black, cavernous hallway. With his hands stretched out in front of him, he went left and navigated through the darkness toward the room where Jaden had to be. Halfway down the long hall, with the emptiness of absolute night all around him, he stopped.

That's when he heard footsteps behind him—heavy ones—coming his way.

CHAPTER FIFTY-FIVE

JOSH FELT NAKED IN the middle of the hallway and knew a set of bathrooms wasn't far away. He eased to his right and felt along the wall, his fingers barely brushing the lockers until he felt the empty space. He ducked into the alcove and crouched down, wedging himself under the drinking fountain. The footsteps came, thunking the floor like horse hooves, closer and closer—and with them the sound of door handles being rattled along the way—until they reached the alcove and stopped.

Josh held his breath. He heard Rocky's lungs filling and the soft wheeze as he breathed out through his nose. Rocky stepped toward him. One step. Two steps. Three.

If Josh reached out, he could have touched Rocky's knee.

Suddenly Rocky slammed his hand into the bathroom

door. The handle rattled as he tried to yank it open, then he turned on his heel and kept going down the hall.

"I know you're here!"

Rocky's voice jolted the darkness and Josh gasped, even though the sound of his footsteps kept going.

"I'm not gonna hurt you," Rocky said, calling out in the empty space. "Not as long as you give me that phone. You give me that phone and we're all set, you and me. Josh, too."

Josh felt his insides melt at the sound of his name spewing from Rocky's lips, but he slipped out of the alcove anyway, following the enormous coach, even though he had no idea what he could do to stop him. Rocky grabbed the handle to a classroom and shook it. Josh could tell by the sound that it was locked. Rocky kept going, crossing the hall and shaking the handle of the next classroom door.

Josh plastered himself against the wall and moved slowly, following Rocky down the long hallway toward the newspaper office. When Rocky finally came to the last door on the left, Josh froze. He heard the hardware click—an open door. But when Rocky went to push it in, something blocked him and a small shriek sounded from within.

Rocky's angry roar exploded in Josh's ears, sending another blast of fear through his frame.

"I know you're here!" Rocky yelled. "Give me that phone!"

By now Josh's eyes had adjusted enough to the darkness that he could make out the vague shape of his hulking coach, and he saw him rear back and swing something.

CRACK!

A baseball bat.

Rocky pounded the door over and over, with Jaden inside, somehow blocking the door shut.

Josh thought she might be okay, that the door would hold.

But just as he thought that, the wood began to splinter.

CHAPTER FIFTY-SIX

A VOICE WAILED INSIDE of Josh, a voice crying out that he should have called the police. If he had, someone might be on the way at that very moment. But he hadn't called, and he couldn't now, and even if he did, it would be too late. He needed something big. Something spectacular.

The idea came to him, and he turned without worrying whether Rocky heard him, sprinting down the hallway, back toward the entrance. When he reached the place where the bathroom was, Josh splayed his fingers and groped along the wall, up and down, side to side, feeling.

At the other end of the hallway, the pounding stopped. Josh heard Rocky climbing through the hole he'd beaten through the door. Then Josh's fingers found what he'd been looking for: the fire alarm.

His fingers gripped the handle and he yanked it down.

Alarm bells shattered his eardrums and safety lights flooded the hallway. Rocky burst from the newspaper office like a bull breaking free from a rodeo chute. Dust and splinters of wood flew into the hallway. Instinctively, Josh ducked into the shadows of the bathroom alcove.

Rocky charged past, running full speed with the metal baseball bat in one hand and with what had to be Jaden's cell phone in the other. He disappeared, and Josh heard the side door smash open as Rocky sprang free into the night.

Josh took off after him without even thinking. He wanted to get outside and call the police. If Benji stopped the car, Rocky wouldn't be able to get away. When Josh reached the entrance he saw Benji standing in the parking lot where he'd left him with the bikes. The Porsche's engine raced. Tires squealed as Rocky shot forward without a hitch. The car rocketed past Josh in a swirl of grit and dust and exhaust.

"Benji!" Josh screamed, clenching both hands and teeth.

Benji held his hands up in the air and flashed Josh a silly smile.

"Jaden," Josh said, suddenly remembering her.

He darted back into the school and down the hallway toward the newspaper office. He coughed at the dust and peered into the old classroom through the huge, jagged hole in the door with his hands over his ears to protect them from the endless clang of the fire bells. A beam of light fell into the room, and Josh saw the tangle of desks Jaden had jammed between the door and the far wall, making it impossible for anyone to get in without smashing a hole in the door.

"Jaden," Josh said, calling her name loudly above the sound of the alarm, his voice laced with panic. "Are you okay?"

Josh saw her dark shape propped up against the leg of the table where the power switch of the printing machine winked at him. He saw movement. If she spoke, he didn't hear her. Her body shook and heaved, and he knew she was silently crying.

"What's wrong?" he shouted, his fright turning to dread. "What happened?"

CHAPTER FIFTY-SEVEN

"ARE YOU HURT?" JOSH said, climbing through the hole, sliding off a desk, and crouching beside her.

Josh put a hand on her shoulder and felt the tremors pass through her. He asked her again and she shook her head, sniffing.

"I gave it to him," she said. He could barely hear the words, but the movement of her lips was clear.

"That's okay," Josh said, hugging her. "It doesn't matter. We tried."

Josh helped her up and through the hole. They both held their ears as they hurried down the hallway for the exit. They dashed out of the school and froze at the sight of flashing lights. Out on the street, two fire trucks and a police car shone their headlights on a car accident, where smoke and flames danced amid a heap of wreckage at the base of the big light pole on

238

the far side of the boulevard.

Jaden took Josh's hand and they crossed the parking lot, hypnotized by the sight. When they reached Benji, he slapped his hands together as though dusting them off.

"You sounded mad at me, dude," Benji said, patting Josh on the back.

"What happened?" Josh asked.

"You thought he got away," Benji said. "I heard it in your voice. Dude, you were so mad at me, but why waste a good bike? Besides, he could have run it over, and unless it got jammed up in the undercarriage, he'd just keep going."

"What happened?" Jaden asked.

The three of them walked toward the flames as the firefighters scrambled with their hose.

Benji held up a ballpoint pen and said, "The pen really *is* mightier than the sword."

"Meathead," Josh said, "what *happened*?"

Benji shrugged and said, "You can't make a turn like that without air in your tires."

"You punctured his tires?" Josh asked, raising his voice above the sound of more sirens heading their way.

"I let the air out," Benji said, grinning widely as they crossed the grass. "You said stop him, and I thought, 'He ain't going anywhere with four flats.'"

They could now see Rocky sitting in the middle of the street, propped up against the front tire of the police car with his head back and his eyes closed.

"Is he okay?" Josh asked the cop who stood by the

back of the patrol car, talking on his cell phone.

"Him?" the cop said. "Yeah. Broke his leg, but nothing fatal. Ambulance is on its way. Hey, do you kids know anything about that fire alarm?"

Another fire truck, sirens wailing, turned off the boulevard and into the school drive.

"You kids shut up!"

They all turned and looked. Rocky glared at them, pointing a thick finger.

"You keep quiet if you know what's good for you. My lawyer will be here to straighten this all out," Rocky said.

"Settle down," the cop said, angling his head toward another cop who had walked over to Rocky.

The first cop herded the three of them over onto the sidewalk, away from the burning Porsche and the broken coach.

"What's he talking about?" the cop asked. "What's going on here?"

"Dude," Benji said to the cop, "I don't know nothing."

Josh and Jaden looked at each other. If they told, it would put an end to Rocky. If they didn't, maybe a good lawyer could sort the whole thing out and both their fathers would be safe.

"What should we do?" Josh asked Jaden.

She closed her eyes, then opened her mouth to speak.

CHAPTER FIFTY-EIGHT

THE POLICE LET THE three of them sit together in a small conference room just off the detectives' squad room, a big, open space full of desks with plainclothes police answering phones and checking their guns before they hurried off. Josh sat at the head of the table with Jaden on one side next to him and Benji on the other. After the patrolmen had questioned them, several detectives came and went, as well as a lieutenant in uniform. One detective, named Fraher, who wore a tweed blazer and tan pants, seemed to be in charge. He had salt-and-pepper hair, rimless glasses, and a red face that changed from cheerful to grim from one moment to the next.

It was late, and Josh, Jaden, and Benji had stopped whispering among themselves. They had moved beyond the fear of what would happen for the crimes they'd committed. Exhaustion weighed them down.

But when Detective Fraher led their parents through the doorway, Josh felt a new surge of anxiety. His sweat glands began to pump, and his mouth dried up in an instant. His father looked enormous as he pushed through the doorway, wearing a dark look beneath his heavy, scowling eyebrows. Josh couldn't read the flat line of his mother's mouth cutting across the width of her pale face. Jaden's father blinked from behind his glasses, looking frightened.

After they all sat down, Detective Fraher placed a cell phone in the middle of the table. Josh and Jaden stared at it.

"That your cell phone?" Fraher asked.

Jaden nodded.

Fraher scooped it up and punched some keys before holding it up and flashing it around the table for everyone to see.

"That the picture?" Fraher asked.

Josh looked from the photo of Dr. Neidermeyer with Rocky to Jaden. She clamped her lips and nodded.

"So," Fraher said, snapping the phone shut and addressing the parents, "you see what they did. We found the drugs and this same bag in Rocky's trunk."

Two uniformed cops came in and stood behind Dr. Neidermeyer, and he stood up between them, still facing Jaden.

Jaden looked up at him, her eyes swimming in tears, and said, "I'm sorry, Dad."

CHAPTER FIFTY-NINE

DR. NEIDERMEYER'S FACE WRINKLED in confusion and he asked, "Why are you sad?"

Jaden shook her head, looking down at her hands, and said, "I was so mad at you for doing this, but now I wish I'd let it be."

"Jaden," Dr. Neidermeyer said, "I taught you to always do the right thing, even if it hurts."

"But you'll go to jail!" she cried.

Dr. Neidermeyer smiled bitterly and shook his head. "Jaden, you don't think I had anything to do with this, do you?"

Jaden's head shot up. She wiped her face and said, "What?"

"You don't think I—" Dr. Neidermeyer said, looking from one police officer to another, scowling. "No, you're wrong, honey. I'm going with them to help. I delivered packages to Rocky Valentine because another doctor asked me to. He knew I always went home through the loading dock, and he started his shift when I ended mine. He's the one who took them. They'll have him on video with it."

Dr. Neidermeyer added, "I thought I was delivering day-old sandwiches from the cafeteria to a homeless guy too ashamed to come out of the shadows. Me give kids steroids?"

Dr. Neidermeyer grimaced, shook his head again, and said, "No, I'm fine, but the doctor doing this isn't going to be. I'm sorry for that, but that was his choice."

"It's true," Detective Fraher said to Jaden.

Jaden shot up out of her chair and ran to her father, hugging him tight. Dr. Neidermeyer blushed and stroked the back of her head.

"You don't think I'm involved with this either, do you, Josh?" his father asked, pointing to his own thick chest.

Josh hung his head and said, "No, not involved, but you knew, right?"

"Josh," his father said in a low rumble, "how could you think that?"

Josh shrugged, looked up at his parents, and said, "All that stuff about being great and doing whatever you have to do."

Josh's father pushed back his chair and came toward him, lifting him out of his chair and squeezing him.

"No, Son," his father said. "Not that. Never that."

His mother moved close and put her hand on Josh's head.

"Well," Fraher said, looking at Benji, "are you going to give me your number now so we can call your parents, or are you still insisting on a lawyer?"

"A lawyer?" Josh's dad said, letting go of Josh and staring down at Benji.

Benji looked up at them, shrugging and raising his hands, and said, "Hey, I saw it on TV."

Josh's father shook his head, snorted, and said to Detective Fraher, "If it's okay with you, we can take him home, Detective."

"I sure don't want him here overnight," Fraher said, getting up from the table and putting Jaden's cell phone into his briefcase before closing it. "I've still got work to do."

"Dad?" Josh asked. "Does this ruin everything? With your job and the Titans and all that?"

His father looked at him, smiled, and said, "You didn't take any of that stuff, did you?"

"No, Dad," Josh said.

"Good," his father said, gripping Josh's shoulder. "If you're healthy and well, then nothing's ruined. It's all good. No, actually, it's great."

CHAPTER SIXTY

The smell of cooking hot dogs floated on the warm summer air. Above, only the wisps of clouds and a hot yellow sun painted the sky's blue field. Josh left the on-deck circle and glanced up at the scoreboard. They were down one run in the bottom of the last inning with two outs.

Word on the other team's relief pitcher was that his dad had pitched for the Cuban national team that won a gold medal in the 1992 Olympics. People said his fastball had more heat than any other U12 player's in the entire country, and he stood a good inch taller than Josh—just over six feet. The only person to get on base since he'd taken the mound was Esch, who'd been hit by a pitch and had to be helped to first base.

Benji passed Josh on his way back to the dugout, his

head hanging after having just struck out.

"It's okay, buddy," Josh said. "I'll get him."

Benji looked up, grinned, and punched him softly in the shoulder. "He was afraid to throw that heat at me, so look for his curveball and watch out for the changeup. He might have gotten the word on both of us—heavy hitters and all."

Josh winked at him and approached the plate.

More people than he'd ever seen filled the stands for the finals of the tournament in the stadium just outside Tampa. The winner would have the chance to play in the Junior Olympics. Up in the seats behind the backstop, Josh waved to his mom and Jaden, who clenched her teeth and held her pen and notebook ready, then he turned his attention to the pitcher and stepped into the box.

Esch cheered him from first base.

From the dugout, his father yelled, "Swing big, buddy!"

Josh wagged his bat, feeling it, and glued his eyes on the pitcher. The spin on the ball said curve, headed low and inside. Josh let it pass.

"Ball!" the umpire cried.

Josh hefted his bat, finding its groove, and readied himself. The pitcher wound up. The ball flew from his hand, laces spinning in a backward blur Josh knew meant heat, right down the middle.

Josh cocked his hips that extra inch and swung big with all he had.

CRACK.

Josh didn't even hurry. He straightened up and jogged down the first-base line, dumping his bat in the grass and watching the ball sail a good fifty feet over the center-field fence. The crowd went crazy. The dugout went crazier. Esch waited for him at home plate along with the rest of the team to carry him around.

Finally they put him down. The two teams shook hands, and the players mixed with the parents and friends who'd spilled out onto the field. Josh saw Jaden and his mom heading his way, grinning. He gave them a thumbs-up and turned away. He found his dad, alone in the dugout, stuffing equipment into the bag. Josh cleared his throat, and his dad looked up and smiled.

"Congratulations, Dad," Josh said. "I mean, Coach."

"That's what I was going to say," a man's voice said from behind him.

Josh spun around. An athletic young man with short blond hair and wearing a black Nike sweat suit stepped forward to shake Josh's dad's hand.

"I'm Mitch Major, Nike's youth baseball rep. I think I might have met you."

Josh's dad's face clouded over and his eyebrows dipped.

"You mean with Rocky Valentine?" Josh's dad asked, his voice a rumble. "I've got nothing to do with him, or all that trouble."

"No," Major said, waving his hand, "forget about

that. He's on his way to jail, right?"

Josh's dad nodded.

"I want to talk about *you*," Major said, "and your team. This is your son, right?"

Josh nodded at Major.

"He's got some bat," Major said, glancing at Josh. "We want to sign up your team. Sponsor the whole thing. The full package, just like we were going to do with Rocky. Coach's salary, all that. What do you think?"

The hard expression on Josh's dad's face melted away and he said, "I think, great."

"And we've got a special program we're starting that I want to get Josh here involved with," Major said. "The way he just stepped up, cool as a carrot under pressure, and knocked that pitch out of the park? I loved that. I want to sign him up, individually."

"What do you mean?" Josh's dad asked, his face darkening again. "He plays for us."

"No, not take him away," Major said. "Just sponsor him. It's a new program. We try to take kids we see from around the country and pay them to be in our ads and give them a bunch of free Nike stuff. Your team will have the stuff anyway. But, hey, they pay pretty good for these ads, and it'll help with college expenses. Even a full scholarship won't cover everything. A kid needs pocket money."

Jaden and Josh's mom appeared at the dugout entrance and his mom said, "College is where he's headed."

Major nodded at her.

"Why do you want *me* in an ad?" Josh asked.

Major laughed at him and said, "Kid, you're more than good. Thing is, what we're trying to find is the next generation, before they're even off the ground. Remember what we did with Tiger Woods? Signed him up before he ever won a dollar. We're gonna do the same thing with baseball."

"And Nike, you, think I'll be *that* good?" Josh asked.

"Kid," Major said, shaking Josh's hand, "from what I've seen, you're on your way to being a baseball great."

35674050001388